"Come on. Let's keep walking."

But before Cody could take even another step forward, something whistled past his ear, followed by the distinctive popping sound of weapons firing.

"Get down!" He shoved Bette into the snow and threw himself on top of her as bullets continued to strike around them. "Into the trees," he said and pushed her forward. Scrambling in the deep snow, they headed for a stand of fir fifty yards to their left, away from the direction of the shots. They moved clumsily through the thick snow, clawing their way toward cover as bullets continued to rain down. Cody tried to keep himself between Bette and the shooter, staying low to present a smaller target and moving erratically when possible.

They had almost reached cover when the impact of a bullet propelled him forward. Burning pain radiated from his shoulder as he fell, but he kept moving, crawling after Bette, into the trees. They lay at the base of one of the evergreens, gasping.

"You're hurt!" Bette stared at his shoulder, her face almost as white as the surrounding snow.

SNOWBOUND SUSPICION

CINDI MYERS

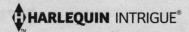

For D'ann

ISBN-13: 978-1-335-64083-3

Snowbound Suspicion

Recycling programs
for this product may
not exist in your area.

Printed in U.S.A.

www.Harlequin.com

Cindi Myers is the author of more than fifty novels. When she's not crafting new romance plots, she enjoys skiing, gardening, cooking, crafting and daydreaming. A lover of small-town life, she lives with her husband and two spoiled dogs in the Colorado mountains.

Books by Cindi Myers

Harlequin Intrigue

Eagle Mountain Murder Mystery: Winter Storm Wedding

Ice Cold Killer
Snowbound Suspicion

Eagle Mountain Murder Mystery

Saved by the Sheriff
Avalanche of Trouble
Deputy Defender
Danger on Dakota Ridge

The Ranger Brigade: Family Secrets

Murder in Black Canyon
Undercover Husband
Manhunt on Mystic Mesa
Soldier's Promise
Missing in Blue Mesa
Stranded with the Suspect

The Men of Search Team Seven

Colorado Crime Scene
Lawman on the Hunt
Christmas Kidnapping
PhD Protector

Visit the Author Profile page at Harlequin.com.

CAST OF CHARACTERS

US Marshal Cody Rankin—On forced leave from his job pursuing fugitives, Cody wrestles with frustration and boredom on his friend's ranch.

Bette Fuller—Excited about catering her best friend's wedding, Bette is trying hard to live down past mistakes.

Lacy Milligan—The bride-to-be is determined not to let snowstorms and a serial killer put a damper on her wedding.

The Ice Cold Killer—The serial killer is targeting women in and around Eagle Mountain and has everyone on edge.

Rainey Whittington—The ranch cook makes it clear she doesn't want Bette around.

Doug Whittington—Rainey's son avoids Bette and joins his mother in trying to make Bette's life miserable.

Eddie Rialto—Bette's former boyfriend ruined her life. Now that he's out of prison, has he decided to make her pay for testifying against him?

Carl Wayland—This friend of Eddie's has shown up in Eagle Mountain and may or may not be stalking Bette.

Chapter One

"More snow forecast today for most of the state, with highs in the mid to upper thirties. Parts of the state could see accumulations of another foot, on top of already record amounts of snow this past week. Travel advisories remain active and avalanche danger remains high."

Bette Fuller switched off the radio and gripped the steering wheel more tightly. White flakes drifted down from the gray sky like glitter in a snow globe—so pretty unless you were the shaken-up person in the middle of the flurry. To the growing list of things she didn't like she added incessant snow. And driving in the mountains on narrow, two-lane roads with no guard rails and steep drop-offs. Flashing lights up ahead made her tense her whole body as she eased her Ford Focus past the Highway Patrol vehicle parked on the side of the road. The patrolman stood in the road, motioning traffic past what appeared to be a large boulder in the middle of the road. Bette averted her eyes and shuddered.

Cops. She didn't like them, either, and she was headed for a whole house full of them. If Lacy Milligan hadn't been one of her best friends in the whole world, she would have turned the car around and headed straight back to Denver. But Lacy was her friend, and it wasn't every day a friend got married. Not to mention, catering this wedding was a really big deal. Whether she liked it or not, Lacy was something of a celebrity in Colorado, and the press was sure to cover her wedding to Sheriff Travis Walker. The irony of that matchup made the media salivate—Lacy was marrying the man who had been instrumental in sending her to prison for a murder she didn't commit. The sheriff had redeemed himself by working to get Lacy released, resulting in a story the press couldn't get enough of.

This could be the big break Bette needed to really get her catering business on solid footing. What was a little snow compared with the opportunity to help a friend and advance her career? She had faced down tougher situations than this before. She hadn't always made good choices in the past, but she was a different person now. This time she was going to succeed.

Twenty minutes later, she drove the Ford underneath the welded iron arches that proclaimed Walking W Ranch, est. 1942, and wound her way down the plowed drive—five-foot walls of snow on each side of the single snowy lane. The drive ended in a cleared parking area, a short distance from a sprawling log-and-stone ranch house. Bette shut off the engine and let out a long breath. She'd made it. With luck, that drive would be the worst part of the whole two and a half weeks she would be here.

She climbed out of the car and stretched, unkinking muscles that had been tensed for most of the snowy drive. This was some place Lacy's fiancé—or rather, his parents—had. It looked like something out of a movie, or some Western lifestyle magazine. The front door of the house opened and a man stepped out onto the porch—a tall man in a cowboy hat and one of those long, leather coats with the cape about the shoulders. What did they call them? *Dusters*, that was the word.

The man in the duster raised a gloved hand and bounded down the steps and strode toward her through the still-falling snow. Her heart hammered painfully as she took in his broad shoulders and long stride. He might be dressed like a cowboy, but his attitude was all cop. She had been around enough of them the last few years to be able to spot that particular I'm-in-charge demeanor from across the yard.

"You must be Bette. Travis said you were supposed to be here today." The man stopped in front of her and offered his hand.

Tentatively, she extended her own hand, only to have it engulfed by his leather-clad paw. A tremor of a different kind traveled through her as her eyes met his steely blue gaze and she silently cursed. Of all the really inconvenient times for her to be reminded that it had been a very long time since she'd been this close to a good-looking man.

"I'm Cody Rankin," he said. "Travis and his brother are at work and I guess Lacy is in town, though she should be up here later today. Travis's sister, Emily, is around somewhere, but at the moment, looks like it's just you and me."

Oh, joy, Bette thought, though she didn't say the words out loud. Not that Cody Rankin wasn't a perfectly nice—and perfectly gorgeous—specimen of manhood. She just didn't want anything to do with charming men right now. Especially one who wore a badge. "Are you one of Travis's cop friends?" she asked. Better to get that part of the introductions over with.

"I'm a US marshal," he said. "Though I'm on vacation right now." He nodded toward the trunk of the car. "Can I help you with your luggage? Though I'm not sure where the Walkers have you staying—maybe one of the guest cabins."

"I'll leave the suitcases in the car until I find out where they want me," she said. "But I have a cooler that needs to go into the house." Before she had left Denver, she'd stocked up on fondant, meringue powder, good Belgian baking chocolate and a handful of other ingredients she wasn't sure she would be able to find out here in the boonies.

"I'll get it." He waited while she popped the trunk, then reached in and hefted out the heavy cooler as if it weighed no more than a box of paper towels.

"How is it you know Lacy?" he asked as he led the way up the walk.

She was glad she was walking behind him, so that he couldn't see the way she stiffened at the question. Of course, she had expected it. It was the kind of thing people asked at weddings: "How do you know the bride?" She just hadn't had a chance to think of a good answer. "We met when we were cellmates in prison" wasn't the kind of answer that went over well in polite company, even though it was the truth.

"We've been friends a long time," she said.

He opened the door and led the way into a

large great room, fire crackling in a woodstove against the back wall, trophy mounts staring down at them from near the log beams overhead. Bette followed Cody through a paneled door into an equally massive kitchen, the marble-topped island in the center of the room as big as a queen-size bed, stainless appliances reflecting the glow of cherry cabinets. He set the cooler in front of a French-door refrigerator and started to open it. "I'll put everything away myself," Bette said, rushing forward. "Thank you."

He straightened. "Okay," he said, then shrugged out of the duster to reveal a snap-button chamois shirt the color of light brown sugar that stretched over impressive shoulders. Well-fitting faded Wranglers and scuffed brown boots completed the outfit. Her gaze shifted to the gun in a holster on his hip. Discreet, but unmistakable. He put a hand to the gun. "I probably don't need this here," he said. "But habits die hard. I'd feel kind of naked without it."

His word choice created a disturbing picture. She turned away, hoping he wouldn't notice her reaction. "How was your drive from Denver?" he asked. "You're lucky you made it through. The pass has been closed."

"I know," she said. "I've been watching for my chance to get here." She leaned back against the kitchen island, arms folded. "The drive wasn't too bad. Are you in the wedding?"

"One of the groomsmen." He reached past her to pluck a grape from a bunch in a bowl on the island and she caught the clean aroma of shaving cream and fabric softener. "I took vacation to come up here early, thinking Travis and I could hang out before he tied the knot—but he's been working overtime on this serial killer case."

"Serial killer? Here?" Eagle Mountain was such a small town, and so remote. What would a serial killer be doing here?

"You didn't know? It's been all over the news."

"I don't pay much attention to the news." She had been too focused on preparing to come here.

"Three women have been murdered so far—one right here on the ranch." He popped a grape in his mouth and crunched down on it. "Be careful if you go anywhere by yourself."

"I'll keep that in mind."

"I'm surprised Lacy didn't mention it to you, but then, maybe she didn't want to frighten you away."

She met his gaze with a hard look of her own. "I don't frighten easily, Marshal Rankin."

"Aw, call me Cody. We're going to be seeing a lot of each other these next two weeks." He popped another grape in his mouth and crunched. "Now that you've arrived, the time here is going to be a lot less dull."

And just what did he mean by that? "I came here to work," she said. Not only had Lacy hired her to cater for the wedding, she was also preparing food for a bridesmaids' tea and the rehearsal dinner.

"If you need a sous chef, I'm your man." He straightened. "Seriously, I'm bored out of my gourd, with Travis working all the time. I'm not used to being this idle. My job is pretty intense, high-energy stuff—pursuing fugitives, most of whom don't want to be caught."

Bette was well aware of what US marshals did—she wasn't likely to ever forget being tackled by one and dragged, handcuffed, into a waiting car. How long into her visit to the ranch before Cody Rankin figured out her history? One phone call to his office was all it would take to get the whole sordid tale. Or he could just ask his friend Travis. Bette assumed Lacy had told her fiancé about her background. Yet he had agreed to let her come to his home and cater his wedding anyway. Now, that was true love.

A door at the opposite end of the room opened, ushering in a blast of cold air and a tall, angular woman wrapped in a blue wool coat. She stopped short upon seeing them. "Marshal Rankin." She nodded to Cody, then her bird-like eyes shifted to Bette. "Who are you?"

"I'm the caterer—Bette Fuller." Bette started around the island toward the woman, but the woman took a step back.

"I'm Rainey," she said. "And I'm in charge of the kitchen here. I told Travis he didn't need to hire a caterer. I'm perfectly capable of providing anything they need in the way of food—I've been doing it for years. But I guess brides these days want to be able to say they've had their wedding 'catered' by a 'chef.'" She sniffed. "Just stay out of my way when it comes to preparing regular meals. I have all the help I need from my son." She looked back over her shoulder. "Doug! Come in here!"

A man Bette judged to be in his late twenties or early thirties, his head engulfed in a fur cap with earflaps, shuffled into the kitchen, half a dozen plastic shopping bags suspended from each hand. He stopped short when he saw Bette. "Hello," he said, his eyes meeting hers, then darting away.

"This is my son, Doug," Rainey said. "He's been to culinary school and plans to open his own restaurant soon, though for the time being he's helping me here at the ranch. The two of us could have provided anything the Walkers need for the wedding."

Well, Bette certainly didn't have to wonder what Rainey thought about her being here. "I'll try to stay out of your way," she said. "I have some things that need to go in the refrigerator." She indicated the cooler.

"Not in here. Put them in the other refrigerator, in the garage." She jerked her head toward a door at the side of the room. "Doug, show her where to put her stuff."

But Doug had disappeared, the back door slamming behind him.

"I'll show you." Cody shrugged back into his duster, then picked up the cooler. "Nice seeing you again, Rainey," he called over his shoulder. "That omelet you made me for breakfast was divine."

Bette said nothing until they were in the garage, in front of an older-model—but still very high-end—refrigerator. She opened the door and surveyed the contents, which appeared to consist mostly of bottles of beer and a large cardboard box labeled Venison Sticks. Cody reached past her and helped himself to one of the sticks, which resembled a very thin frankfurter. "These are excellent," he said, tearing open the wrapper. "Travis's dad makes them, from venison he harvests himself."

Bette nodded and rearranged some of the beer bottles to make room for her chocolate and fondant. "I can see dealing with Rainey is going to be a barrel of laughs."

"Ignore her." Cody held the top of the cooler open for her. "Lacy and Travis want you here, and that's all that matters."

"Oh, I won't let her get to me," Bette said. "I've dealt with worse." Some of the guards at the Denver Women's Correctional Facility would have made Rainey look like a creampuff. She stowed the last of the items in the refrigerator and shut the door. "Are Mr. and Mrs. Walker around? I'd like to find out where I'm staying."

"They headed to Junction while the pass is open," Cody said. "Rainey might know." He looked doubtful.

Bette laughed. "If it was up to her, she'd put me in a horse stall or something." She shut the lid of the cooler. "No, I can wait until Lacy shows up."

She started to pick up the empty cooler, but Cody swiped it from her. She shrugged. If he wanted to tote her belongings for her, let him. It didn't mean she owed him anything.

Instead of heading back into the kitchen, he led the way out of the garage and around to the front of the house. "Okay if I leave the cooler out here?" he asked, indicating a spot on the covered front porch near the door.

"That's fine." She started to open the door but stilled at the sound of a car approaching. A red Jeep zipped into a parking place near the house. The driver's door flew open and Lacy Milligan, her dark hair in short layers around her face and topped by a pink fleece cap with an oversize pom-pom like the tail of a rabbit, her petite frame wrapped in a white puffy coat that reached to the top of her fur-trimmed boots, raced toward them, arms outstretched.

"Bette!" Lacy squealed and grabbed her friend in a crushing hug. "Oh, it's so good to see you! How have you been? Was the drive from Denver horrible? Oh, let me look at you." She released her hold on Bette and took a step back. "You look fantastic. Oh, I'm so glad you're here."

"You look great yourself," Bette said. She couldn't stop grinning. Just being with Lacy again made her happy.

"I've been trying to make her feel welcome." Cody spoke up from his spot just behind Bette.

"Thank you, Cody," Lacy nodded to him, then turned back to Bette. "I'm sorry I wasn't here when you arrived. With the wedding less than three weeks away things are absolutely crazy. And with the road being closed and Travis working so much—I swear, I'm going to need a vacation when this is over."

She took Bette's arm and ushered her into the house. "I'm going to head over to the stables, if anyone needs me," Cody said, but Bette doubted Lacy heard. She was chattering away about the wedding preparations and the snow and Travis and who knew what else. Bette glanced behind her to watch Cody exit, his duster slung over one arm.

"Leave it to you to make friends with the best-looking single man in the place." Lacy nudged Bette. "It's a good thing you weren't around when I reconnected with Travis. He wouldn't have looked twice at me."

"I'm not interested in catching the eye of any man," Bette said. "That's how I got into so much trouble in the first place, remember?"

Lacy's expression clouded. "You don't hear from Eddie anymore, do you?"

Bette shook her head. "No. And I hope I never do." Hooking up with Eddie Rialto had been the absolute worst decision she had ever made in her life. "I'm staying happily single from now on."

"Oh, men aren't all bad," Lacy said. "You just have to meet the right one."

"You're in love, so you think everyone else should be, too," Bette said. "That's sweet, but

I'm here to work—and to spend time with you and wish you well. That's plenty to keep me occupied."

"And I'm so glad you're here." Lacy took both of Bette's hands in her own and lowered her voice, her expression serious. "Have you met Rainey yet?"

"Oh, yes, I met Rainey."

Lacy winced. "I'm sorry I didn't warn you. She can be a real grouch, but I guess she's worked for the Walker family forever, so I try not to say anything. She wanted to cook for the wedding herself, but thank goodness Travis backed me up when I said I wanted to hire you."

"I really appreciate your giving me this chance." Bette squeezed Lacy's hands, then released them. "But tell me the truth—how many people know about me? How many people know the two of us met in prison?"

"Travis knows, of course. And his parents. I had to tell them. And his brother, Gage, probably knows. I don't think he and Travis have any secrets. But it doesn't matter. They know you served your time and paid for your mistakes, and that you're making a fresh start. They admire you for it, the way I do. And really, what can they say? I was in prison, after all."

"You were innocent," Bette said. "And Travis proved it. You never did the things you were convicted for. But I was guilty. I did help rob a bank."

"You made a mistake and you paid for it," Lacy repeated. "That doesn't mean you're a bad person."

Bette let out a breath, trying to ease the tension in her neck. "I'm glad Travis and his parents were so understanding." She glanced toward the door. "Not everyone would be."

"If you're thinking of Cody, I'm sure he doesn't know," Lacy said. "And Rainey doesn't know, so don't worry about her. Did you meet Doug?"

"We were introduced. He didn't stick around long."

"Just so you know, he has a record, too. He's supposedly reformed, but frankly, he gives me the creeps. Rainey won't hear a word against him, though, so if I were you, I'd have nothing but good things to say about her darling boy. You'll get on her best side that way."

"Does she have a best side?"

Both women laughed. Lacy put her arm around Bette. "We have you staying in one of the guest cabins," she said. "It's adorable, plus you'll have your privacy. Come on, I'll show you. And then I want a nice long visit, so I can hear all about what you've been up to."

Chapter Two

Cody leaned over the stall to run his hand along the rough velvet of the mare's shoulder, and smiled as the animal nuzzled at his shirt pocket. "Sorry, girl, I don't have any treats for you today," he said. He'd have to remember to bring a few horse nuggets or a carrot with him next time he visited the stables.

The mare lost interest and turned away to pull hay from the rack on the wall and Cody sat on the feed bin across from the stall. He inhaled deeply of the oats-and-molasses aroma of sweet feed and the still-green scent of hay, and tried to quiet his racing mind. He'd been spending a lot of time here since coming to the ranch. The stables were a quiet place to think. Or maybe *brood* would be a better word. He wanted to be out there, tracking down and apprehending fugitives, getting bad guys off the streets. Instead, his supervisors had forced him into taking vacation. One screw-up and they thought the answer was time off, but they were wrong. He needed to be back out in the field, proving to them and to himself that he could still handle the job.

He hadn't minded so much about the forced leave at first—he'd figured this would be a good chance for him and Travis to catch up before the wedding. They could go ice fishing, or maybe elk hunting. Cody could help with work on the ranch. Instead, Travis was neck-deep in the hunt for a serial killer, and Cody could do nothing to help. Sure, his friend had taken pity and let him sit in on a few briefings, but Cody had no jurisdiction and, really, no experience figuring out who committed crimes. As a US marshal, his job was to find the suspects after they had been identified.

At least he wouldn't be the only outsider at the ranch now. Bette Fuller had been a nice surprise. Somehow, when Travis had talked about the caterer, Cody had pictured an older woman—maybe someone who looked like Julia Child. Instead, a curvy blonde with the most amazing blue eyes and a full mouth that smiled with a hint of a challenge had emerged from the snowstorm to make life on the ranch a whole lot more interesting.

She hadn't exactly warmed up to Cody. Was Bette so cool to him because he was a cop, or a man—or both? Never mind—he liked a challenge, and they had a couple of weeks to get to know each other better. And if they did hit it off, she was from Denver, and so was he. This could be the start of a fun friendship.

He stood. Time to head back to the house. Bette and Lacy should have had enough time to swap girl talk, and maybe he could find out from Lacy what was up with Travis. As he exited the stables, the scent of tobacco smoke drifted to him. He followed the smell around the side of the barn, where he found Doug Whittington, huddled out of the wind, with a half-smoked cigarette. "Hello, Doug," he said.

The young man jumped and made as if to hide the cigarette behind his back. "Too late for that." Cody joined him in the L formed by the stables and the tack room. "I don't care if you smoke—just don't set the barns on fire."

"Don't tell my mother," Doug said, then took another long drag. In his late twenties or early thirties, he had close-cropped brown hair and freckles. Cody had never seen him smile, and probably hadn't exchanged a dozen words with him in the week since he had arrived at the ranch.

Neither man said anything as Doug finished the cigarette. He threw down the butt and ground it into the snow with the heel of his boot. "Who's that girl?" he asked. "The one who showed up today."

"You mean Bette?" Was Doug asking because he was interested in the pretty newcomer? Cody couldn't blame the guy, though he didn't think the sullen cook was the type to catch the eye of someone like Bette. "She's catering the wedding."

"Yeah, but who is she? Where's she from and who decided she should come here?"

"She's from Denver and she's a friend of Lacy's."

"Did you know her in Denver?"

"No. Why did you think that?"

"The two of you seemed friendly, that's all."

Cody laughed. He wouldn't have called his interaction with Bette exactly friendly. "Are you worried she might take your mother's job?" he asked. "I don't think that's her intention at all."

Doug rolled his shoulders. "Just wondering. How long is she going to be here?"

"The wedding is in two and a half weeks, so I imagine she'll be here at least until then."

"Just wondering," he said again, then stuffed his hands in his pockets. "I gotta go."

He shuffled off through the snow, away from the house. He was an odd duck, Cody thought, but then, it took all kinds. He headed back to the house and found Lacy and Bette seated before the fire. "Cody!" Lacy greeted him with her usual enthusiasm. "We wondered where you had gone off to."

"I thought I'd give you two a little time alone to catch up," he said. He took a seat at the end of the sofa on one side of the woodstove, opposite Bette.

"So considerate," Lacy said. "Have you been bored out of your mind up here by yourself? I hope not."

"I'm okay," he said. "How's Travis? Any word on how the case is going?"

Lacy shook her head. "I saw him for a few minutes this afternoon, but you know him—he doesn't like to talk about cases. He did say he'd try to make it home for dinner."

"Being a cop's wife isn't for the faint of heart," Cody said.

"Oh, I know that." Lacy waved off his concern. "But I love Travis as much for what he does as for who he is. I like that he's so committed to doing what's right. If he wasn't, I'd still be sitting in prison."

Cody still marveled that Travis had ended up marrying a woman he had arrested for murder. Three years after her conviction, the sheriff had discovered new evidence that proved Lacy was innocent, and he had thrown himself into seeing that her conviction was vacated. After she was freed, he had enlisted her help to find the real murderer. Talk about an unlikely love story.

"I can't believe there's a serial killer in Eagle Mountain," Bette said. "Lacy, why didn't you tell me?"

"I didn't want to scare you off," Lacy said. "Call me selfish, but it's true." She leaned toward her friend. "You're not scared, are you? You don't need to be. I can't think of anything safer than being here at the ranch, with two lawmen in residence, now that Cody is staying here. And Gage is up here all the time, too."

"I'm not afraid," Bette said. "Though Cody said one of the women was killed here on the ranch."

Lacy frowned. "Well, yes, but that doesn't mean it was someone from here. We were having a scavenger hunt. People were spread out all over the place, so the killer could have sneaked onto the property at any time. But if you make it a point not to go anywhere by yourself, you should be fine."

"I'm happy to accompany you if you need an escort," Cody said, but the offer only earned him a sour look from Bette.

The door from the kitchen opened and Rainey emerged, bearing a large silver tray. Cody rose to help her, but she shrugged him away. "I can get it," she said, as she set the tray on the low table in front of the sofa. "I thought you might like something to snack on before supper."

"Oh, it looks delicious," Lacy said, scooting forward and helping herself to a cheese puff.

Rainey remained tight-lipped. "Have you seen Doug?" she asked. "He's disappeared and it's time for him to help me with supper."

"I saw him a few minutes ago, out by the stables," Cody said.

"Probably smoking a cigarette," Rainey said. "He does that when he's upset."

Cody stuffed a sausage roll into his mouth, using it as an excuse not to comment.

"I can help you if you like," Bette said. She started to stand. "Just tell me what you want me to do."

"I can manage fine on my own," Rainey said. "I've been doing it for years. I'm sure you're the reason Doug is staying away. You've upset him."

"What have I done to upset him?" Bette asked, but Rainey was already walking away, back to the kitchen.

"I'm sorry she's being so rude to you," Lacy said. "I can talk to Mr. and Mrs. Walker if you like. I'm sure they would speak to her."

"No, don't say anything. I don't want to

cause trouble." She stood. "I think what I'd like to do is freshen up before dinner. And I want to check out that cute cabin where you've put me. I didn't see much when we dropped off my luggage."

Cody stood. "Let me walk you out. My cabin isn't far and I should probably clean up before dinner, too."

"I don't think that's really necessary," she said.

"Humor me," he said, lifting her coat off the pegs by the door.

"Let him go with you," Lacy said. "I mean, you're probably perfectly fine, but until Travis catches this killer, it probably doesn't hurt to be overly cautious."

If looks could kill, Cody thought Lacy might have been at least injured by the glare Bette sent her, but she allowed Cody to help her into her coat, and she stalked out the door in front of him.

Cody followed, not trying to catch up with her, more amused than insulted. He half suspected Lacy of doing a little matchmaking, trying to throw the two of them together, but it probably didn't hurt for the women to be a little more careful until the murderer was caught.

Bette had been assigned the first in a row of four log guest cabins arranged alongside the creek, past the horse barns. Cody's cabin was next to hers, the other two reserved for wedding guests due to arrive later. Someone—one of the ranch hands, probably—had shoveled the stone walkway leading to the cabin, which, if it was like Cody's, consisted of a single large room and attached bathroom, and a small covered porch with a single chair and small table.

The sun had set, casting the world around them in gray twilight, but a light shone over the door of Bette's cabin. She stopped at the bottom of the steps leading up onto the porch. Cody halted behind her. "What is it?" he asked, then followed her gaze to the door. There, in bright red paint, someone had scrawled the words *Go Home!*

ONCE SHE WAS over the initial shock of seeing the message on her door, Bette was more angry than frightened. "I guess we know what Doug Whittington was up to when his mother couldn't find him," she said, starting up the steps, her key in her hand.

"Don't touch the door." Cody took her hand as she was reaching for the knob.

She glared at him. "What? You think you're going to find fingerprints? And then what? I don't think a nasty message is exactly a major crime." She pulled out of his grasp, inserted her key in the lock and shoved open the door. Not waiting to be asked, Cody followed her in—not that that surprised her. He was in full-on cop mode, on the case. Except there was no case.

"You don't know that Doug did this," he said.

"Unless his mother took a break from preparing dinner and ran out here with a can of red paint, my money is on Doug. No one else here is so anxious for me to leave." She looked around the room, but clearly nothing had been disturbed. Her unopened suitcases stood by the bed, which was still neatly made, a blue-and-yellow patchwork quilt draped across it.

"I'll talk to him," Cody said.

"No." She grabbed his wrist, squeezing hard, making sure she had his full attention. "Don't say anything. The best way to deal with this kind of harassment is to ignore it."

He set his jaw in a stubborn line and his eyes met hers—denim-blue eyes a woman could get lost in. Clearly, he wasn't a man who ignored anything. "If I tell him to lay off hassling you or he'll have to deal with me, I think he'll stop," he said.

"Your job is not to protect me," she said. "I'm perfectly capable of looking after myself."

He took a step toward her, so that the front of his duster almost brushed against her puffy coat. He was breathing hard, and she realized she was, too. She was torn between wanting to slap him and wanting to grab his shoulders and pull him down to her in a kiss. Her hormones were jumping up and down, shouting, "Big, sexy man—must have," trying hard to drown out her brain, which was pleading that she had more sense than this.

Cody's gaze shifted to her lips and she wondered if he was thinking the same thing—a dangerous thought that had her releasing her hold on him and stepping back, until she bumped into the bed. "You need to leave," she said, her brain momentarily getting the upper hand.

"Yeah, I probably do." He stepped back also, though his eyes remained locked to hers. "Just promise me if anything else happens—something more than annoying messages—you'll call for me. My cabin is next door." He nodded to his right.

"Sure." She hugged her coat more tightly around her body. "But nothing is going to happen. This is kid stuff."

"What are you going to do about the door?"

"I'll find something to clean the message off the door before anyone sees it."

"Or you could show it to the Walkers and let them know what's going on."

"No. I don't want to do anything to upset

them. They've got enough on their hands, between the wedding and this whole serial killer thing. I mean, it can't be that easy, having two sons out hunting a murderer."

Cody wanted to argue—she could practically see the words building up in his head. She braced herself to reply, but instead, he turned and took hold of the doorknob. "Have it your way. But remember—I'm right next door if you need me."

He left and she dropped onto the bed, struggling to control her racing heart. Great. He was next door. Entirely too close for comfort. He had no idea, but Cody Rankin was a lot more dangerous to Bette's well-being than Rainey and her son.

Chapter Three

Bette couldn't decide if the dinner of roast beef, potatoes au gratin, green beans almandine and homemade rolls was designed to impress her with Rainey's prowess in the kitchen, or if it was simply the way the Walker family ate every evening. Add in the gleaming oak table, polished silver and dishes she guessed were hand painted, and the place screamed laid-back luxury. "Everything is so delicious," she said, determined to give credit where credit was due.

"I wish Travis and Gage could have been here," Mrs. Walker said, as she passed the dish of potatoes.

"They said they were sorry to miss eating with us, but they think they have a break in the case," Lacy said.

"I hope that means they're close to catching the murderer," Mrs. Walker said.

"And without another woman dying," Mr. Walker said.

Silence descended on the table, broken only by the clink of ice in glasses and the scrape of forks on china.

"Not the most cheerful topic of conversation," Travis's sister, Emily, said, slicing into her roast.

"One of the hazards of living with law enforcement," Cody said. "Lacy will get used to it."

"Oh, I am," Lacy said. "I think it's interesting, actually."

Mrs. Walker turned to Bette. "I hope you're finding the cabin comfortable."

"Oh, yes," Bette said. "It's beautiful. I'm going to really enjoy staying there."

"Well, if you need anything, just let me know," Mrs. Walker said.

"Maybe some more cleaner." Seated next to her, Cody whispered the words under his breath. Bette kicked him in the shin. She had refused his offer to help scrub the painted message off the front door, but it was true she had used most of a bottle of cleaner and probably ruined a bath towel cleaning everything up. Someone looking closely would probably still be able to see the shadow of the words, but tomorrow she planned to make a wreath or something to hang on the door to cover them up. She had gotten to be pretty crafty, all those years behind bars.

"If I wasn't staying here, you could have had my room," Lacy said. "Though you'll probably appreciate the privacy of the cabin."

"I thought you had a place in town," Bette said. She remembered Lacy's excitement over the apartment she had rented from a friend.

"I do, but Travis persuaded me that I should stay here until the wedding."

"He didn't like the idea of you living alone while this killer is on the loose," Mrs. Walker said. "And I don't blame him."

"It's very sweet of you to take me in," Lacy said. "My room is very nice."

"We thought about putting you in one of the cabins," Mr. Walker said. "But we didn't want to make it too easy for Travis to sneak off to see you. It's good for young men to have a challenge."

Lacy blushed bright pink, while the rest of the table burst into laughter.

The door from the kitchen opened and Rainey entered. "Does anyone need anything?" she asked, surveying the table.

"Everything is delicious," Bette said. "I'll have to get your recipe for the roast—it's so well-seasoned."

"I don't give out my recipes," Rainey said.

Bette kept a smile on her face. She wasn't going to let this old bat get her down.

"My favorite is the potatoes," Cody said.

"Doug made those," Rainey said.

"So I guess he made it back in time to help you with the cooking after all," Cody said.

"I told you, he was just out smoking." She turned on her heels and left them.

"I'm afraid Rainey's feelings are a little hurt that Travis and Lacy didn't ask her to cater the wedding," Mrs. Walker said. "I tried to explain we didn't want to burden her with so much work—and that it meant a lot to Lacy to have her friend do the job. I'm sure she'll calm down soon. In the meantime, I hope you won't let her bother you, Bette."

"Of course not." Bette took a sip of her water, aware of Cody watching her. Honestly, did he have to sit right next to her? She couldn't make a move without being aware of him. When he reached past her for the rolls, his arm brushed hers and a tremor shuddered through her. So annoying. Tomorrow, she'd suggest she trade places at dinner with Lacy or Emily. Or maybe she could stick Travis next to his friend.

"What's next on the wedding agenda?" Emily asked.

"The bridesmaids' tea is Saturday," Lacy

said. "Now that Bette is here, we can finish planning that."

"It sounds very formal," Cody said.

"It's just a chance for us to dress up and eat lots of fancy finger food," Lacy said. "I wanted something different from a bar crawl."

"There aren't many bars to crawl to in Eagle Mountain," Emily said.

"That's not going to stop the men." Lacy looked down the table to Cody. "Gage told me he's planning to kidnap Travis and force him to attend his bachelor party Saturday night."

"If the roads stay open, he's booked a hotel in Junction," Cody said. "If not, we'll make do with Moe's Pub."

"I'm rooting for Moe's," Lacy said. "There's no way they can get into trouble there, with half the town watching them."

Rainey returned and began clearing the table. "Where's Doug?" Cody asked. "Doesn't he usually help you with that?"

"He wasn't feeling well," Rainey said. "I sent him to lie down."

"Let me help." Bette stood and began gathering the plates on her side of the table.

"There's no need for that," Rainey said. "I can manage on my own."

"I want to help," Bette said.

Cody stood and began collecting dishes also. "I'll help, too," he said.

The two of them followed Rainey into the kitchen. "Put the dishes in the sink and then go sit down," Rainey directed. "I don't like a lot of other people in my kitchen while I'm trying to work."

"I'm the same way," Bette said. "You know just where everything is and how you want to do things, and it's annoying to have to keep stopping and telling other people what to do."

Rainey glared at her, but Bette kept smiling.

"I don't think your plan to win her over with flattery and kindness is going to work," Cody whispered as they made their way back to the table.

"Maybe I'm not trying to win her over," Bette said. "Maybe I'm trying to drive her crazy. Crabby people hate it when their enemies are nice to them."

A few moments later, Rainey entered the dining room, carrying a large apple pie and a carton of vanilla ice cream. She set them in the center of the table. "You can serve yourselves," she said.

"None for me." Lacy stood. "I have a wedding dress to fit into."

"Thank goodness, I don't." Bette picked up

the knife and prepared to cut into the pie. "Who wants ice cream?"

Mrs. Walker declined, but everyone else wanted dessert. Bette dished up the pie, while Cody took charge of the ice cream. When everyone was served, Bette sat back and took a bite.

"What do you think?" Cody asked.

"It's very good." She took a small spoonful of ice cream. "A little sweeter than I like, and a dash more of cloves would have been a good addition—but very good."

Lacy, who had left the room, returned, phone in hand. "I just had a text from Adelaide Kinkaid." She glanced at Bette. "She's Travis's office manager."

"Is something wrong with Gage or Travis?" White-faced, Mrs. Walker half rose from her chair.

"They're both fine," Emily said. She studied her phone screen. "Adelaide says they've made an arrest in the Ice Cold Killer case."

"The Ice Cold Killer?" Bette asked.

"That's what they're calling the serial killer," Emily said. "Apparently, he leaves behind little cards—like business cards—that say 'ice cold.'"

"Who did they arrest?" Mrs. Walker asked, settling into her chair once more.

"I texted back that question," Lacy said.

The phone pinged and Lacy swiped the screen. Her eyes widened. "She says they arrested Ken Rutledge."

"Who is Ken Rutledge?" Cody asked.

"He's a schoolteacher," Lacy said. "He lives in the other half of the duplex where Kelly Farrow—the first murder victim—lived."

"So he's the serial killer?" Emily asked.

Lacy shook her head. "Adelaide doesn't say. She just says Travis arrested Ken and Gage and Dwight are driving him to the lockup in Junction tonight."

"Well, she can't say, can she?" Emily asked. "But if Travis arrested him—and he's really connected with the case—then he must be the murderer."

"This whole situation has been horrible," Mrs. Walker said. "But I hope it's over now."

"I do, too," Emily said. "In any case, I know I'll sleep better tonight, knowing a killer is behind bars."

"Speaking of sleeping…" Bette pushed back her chair. "I'm going to say good-night now. I still have to unpack, and I've had a very long day."

"The drive from Denver is enough to wear anyone out," Mrs. Walker said.

"I'll walk you to your cabin." Cody stood also.

"I don't need an escort," Bette said.

She could see in his eyes that he wanted to protest, but she didn't give him a chance. She hurried to hug Lacy, said good-night to the others and quickly made her way to the front door. To her relief, Cody didn't follow.

As she took the shoveled path toward the cabins, she told herself she really didn't have to run away from Cody Rankin. He was just another man, and she was a strong enough woman to resist his attractions.

Maybe she should go ahead and tell him she had a record. As a cop who devoted his life to putting away people like her, that information was sure to make him keep his distance.

CODY WAITED UP with the Walkers until Travis came home. The Rayford County sheriff looked as sharp-pressed and alert as always, though Cody recognized the fatigue in his eyes.

"Well?" he asked, once Travis had shed his coat and kissed Lacy.

"Well what?" Travis asked, his arm around Lacy.

"Is Ken Rutledge the Ice Cold Killer?" Lacy asked.

"Probably not—though we're still tracing his movements around the time of all the murders."

"If he's not the killer, why did you arrest him?" Mrs. Walker asked.

"He attacked Darcy Marsh."

"Darcy is a local veterinarian," Emily told Cody. "She and Kelly Farrow were business partners."

"But you don't think he's the serial killer?" Mrs. Walker asked.

"We're not ruling that out completely." Travis moved past them, toward the fire. "I really can't talk about the case—except I'm wondering how you all already know about the arrest."

"Adelaide texted me," Emily said.

"Of course she did." Travis settled onto the sofa.

"She wanted me to know you were all right," Emily said. "And it's not as if something like that is going to stay a secret very long. I imagine most of the town knows about it by now."

"I imagine they do," Travis said, without anger.

"Did you have anything to eat?" Mrs. Walker asked.

Travis shook his head. "I'll get something in a minute. Right now, I just want to rest and warm up."

"What's the weather like?" Mr. Walker took a seat across from his son.

"It's snowing again. I told Gage and Dwight

to hurry to get the evidence we collected to Junction. If one of the avalanche chutes on Dixon Pass lets loose, they'll have to close the road again."

"You'll be in big trouble if two of your officers get trapped on the other side of the pass," Cody said. "You might even have to deputize me."

"Only as a last resort," Travis said. He didn't smile, but Cody caught the glint of humor in his eye.

"Bette arrived this afternoon," Lacy said. "She's in the first guest cabin. Poor woman was exhausted from the drive." She squeezed Travis's arm. "I can't wait for you to meet her."

"I'm looking forward to it," Travis said, though he didn't sound very enthusiastic. In fact, to Cody's ears, his friend sounded like a man who was telling his fiancée what she wanted to hear, not what he necessarily felt.

Rainey appeared, carrying a tray, which she set on the coffee table in front of Travis. "I've been keeping this warm for you," she said. "Eat it now before it gets cold." Before he could reply, she had turned and fled.

"I see Rainey is in one of her moods tonight," he said. He leaned forward and picked up a fork.

"Her nose is out of joint because Bette is

here," Lacy said. "But honestly, Bette is the nicest person in the world. If anyone can win over Rainey, she can."

"She doesn't have to win her over," Travis said. "She just has to ignore her and cater the wedding."

"Oh, Bette will do a good job," Lacy said. "A wonderful job. And she really appreciates us giving her this chance. It means a lot to her."

"Happy to help." Travis focused his attention on his plate. "I'm starving."

Mr. and Mrs. Walker said good-night, as did Emily, leaving Lacy and Cody alone with Travis. He was wondering if he should leave the couple to themselves when Travis said, "It would make it easy on everyone if Ken Rutledge turns out to be our killer. But I really don't think he is."

"What happened tonight?" Cody asked. "That is, if you think you can talk about it."

"I can talk about it to you." He turned to look at Lacy.

"You know I won't say anything to anyone," she said. "And this is your life. I have to be a part of it."

Travis nodded and looked thoughtful as he chewed, then swallowed. "Someone has been harassing Darcy since Kelly was killed," he said. "Someone ran her off the road, and someone attacked her and Highway Patrolman Ryder Stewart while they were skiing yesterday. Apparently, Rutledge was trying to frighten Darcy into turning to him for help. I think he saw his opportunity when Kelly and Christy O'Brien were murdered, but he went too far."

"You say he attacked Darcy again tonight?" Lacy asked.

"He kidnapped her. Ryder spotted the damaged snowmobile at Ken's duplex and figured out he was the man who had attacked him and Darcy. He found them at Darcy's house and rescued her."

"Why do you think he didn't kill the other women?" Cody asked.

"He has alibis for two of the killings. Pretty solid ones. And while he was willing to admit everything he had done to Darcy, he's adamant that he didn't have anything to do with the murders. We'll see." He pushed his empty plate away and stretched his arms over his head. "I need a shower and bed," he said.

Cody stood. "Good night. See you in the morning."

After the warmth of the fire, the cold hit him like a slap. He hurried along the path to the cabins, his breath fogging in front of his face, snow squeaking under his boots. As he neared the first cabin in the row—Bette's cabin—

movement on the little porch caught his eye. He stopped and stared at the dark shape near the door of the cabin. He moved off the path and took shelter behind a tree. The shape on the porch didn't flee or move toward him—maybe it hadn't seen him coming.

No lights showed behind the cabin's drawn blinds. Bette was probably asleep, unaware that someone was outside her door—and clearly up to no good. Stealthily, using the cover of the trees, Cody moved closer to the cabin. The shape on the porch shifted slightly but didn't leave its position by the door. The shadow wasn't tall enough to be someone standing— Cody thought the man was crouching by the door, perhaps trying to jimmy the lock.

Reaching the end of the porch, Cody didn't hesitate. He made a flying leap and tackled the lurker, forcing him to the ground.

"Let go of me, you creep." An elbow thrust hard into his ribs, followed by nails raked across his face. "Get off of me!" The voice— definitely not a man's—demanded.

Cody couldn't get off fast enough. The beam of a flashlight blinded him. "Cody Rankin!" Bette said. "What do you think you're doing?"

Chapter Four

Cody held up a hand to shield his eyes and took another step back from an enraged Bette. "I saw someone on the porch and thought they were trying to break into your cabin," he said.

"I couldn't sleep and I was sitting out here, enjoying the moonlight." She gathered what appeared to be the quilt from her bed around her. A knit hat covered most of her blond hair, and thick gloves on her hands had probably prevented her from doing more damage to his face.

"It's zero degrees out," he said. "Who sits outside in that kind of weather?"

"It's not bad if you're wrapped up," she said.

He was feeling more foolish by the minute. "I'm sorry," he said. "I didn't hurt you, did I?"

She lowered the light so that it was no longer shining in his eyes. "You scared me half to death, but I'm not hurt. What about you?"

He rubbed his side. "My ribs are going to be sore for a few days, I think."

"Serves you right. Who appointed you my personal protector, anyway?"

"I was on my way back to my cabin and I saw someone lurking on your porch. Someone I didn't think should be there. And protecting people is what I do."

"No, you pursue them."

"I pursue bad guys as a way of protecting law-abiding citizens," he countered.

"Well, you can stop pursuing me."

He started to argue that he wasn't pursuing her, but he was tired of standing out here in the freezing cold. "I'm going to bed," he said, and limped past her.

"You are hurt!" She touched his shoulder, stopping him.

"I've dealt with worse."

"Sure you have, tough guy." She wrapped both hands around his biceps. "Come inside and let me have a look. You might have broken ribs."

He let her lead him into her cabin. Inside, warmth wrapped around him like a cocoon. He sank into the single armchair while she went around turning on lights. She dropped the quilt back onto the bed and divested herself of hat and gloves, revealing herself dressed in knit leggings and a long sweater that clung to every curve. "Take off your jacket and pull up your shirt so I can check your ribs," she said.

He took off the jacket, then took off the shirt, as well. When she turned toward him again he was standing beside the chair, naked from the waist up, and enjoying seeing her flustered. "I didn't tell you to get undressed," she said, avoiding his gaze.

"It's easier this way." He held his arms out to his sides, wincing only a little from the effort.

She moved closer and, after a brief hesitation, felt gently along his rib cage, where a faint bruise was already starting to show. Now it was his turn to be unsettled, the silken touch of her hand sending a jolt of desire straight to his groin. He shifted, trying to get comfortable in an impossibly uncomfortable situation.

She looked up, her eyes soft with concern. "I'm sorry. Did that hurt?"

"No." He took a step back. It was either that or pull her into his arms and kiss her until she was as hot and breathless as he felt. Or until she punched him in the mouth for presuming too much. He reached for his shirt. "I'll be fine," he said. "A little sore, but I guess that's no more than I deserve." He turned away, trying to hide his arousal. "I'll just use your bathroom, then say good-night."

In the bathroom, he splashed cold water on

his face and practiced deep breathing until he had himself under control. Unfortunately, every breath pulled in the soft, feminine scent of Bette's perfume, which did little to lessen his arousal. For whatever reason, Bette Fuller checked every box on his list. His head could tell him to play it cool and keep his distance, but his body was determined to go full-on caveman.

He looked around for a towel on which to dry his hands and wipe his face. Finding none, he opened the cabinet beneath the sink. He spotted a stack of hand towels, but as he reached for one, his hand knocked against something. Crouching and peering into the cabinet, he spotted a paintbrush—and a can of red paint.

The same crimson color that had been used to paint the warning message on her cabin door.

BETTE PACED WHILE Cody was in the bathroom, trying desperately to cool down and calm herself and act like a sensible woman instead of some sex-starved maniac. The sight of Cody Rankin, all six-pack abs and muscular chest, was one that would haunt her dreams—and her fantasies—for no doubt years to come. She wouldn't have been surprised if she had seared her fingers touching him—he was that hot.

And she was in so much trouble if she even

thought about fulfilling the fantasies he inspired. She had lost her head over a man like this before, and he had come close to ruining her life. She didn't put Cody in the same category as Eddie, but he had the same potential to distract her from her goals and make her act recklessly.

The door to the bathroom opened and he emerged—fully dressed and looking grim. Obviously, she had injured him worse than she thought. She straightened. She wasn't going to feel remorse over that. He deserved a little pain for tackling her like that.

She expected him to head for the door, but instead, he sat in the chair again. "Tell me a little more about yourself," he said. "How, exactly, do you know Lacy?"

She frowned. She was tired, it was late and this was no time for a get-to-know-all-about-each-other conversation. Then again, she had been looking for a way to put some distance between herself and this sexy cop. The truth was sure to do that.

She sat on the end of the bed and pulled one end of the quilt across her lap. "We were cellmates in prison." She kept her head up, defiant. She wasn't proud of what she'd done, but she wasn't going to deny it, either.

He blinked. Clearly, he hadn't expected that

one. She waited, then he asked the question she had known would come next. "What were you doing in prison?" he asked.

"Ten years for robbing the bank where I worked as a teller," she said. "Though I was paroled early because I was such a model prisoner."

His eyes narrowed. "So you admit you're guilty."

"Oh, yes. There were five of us—four of us were caught. I was the person on the inside. It was the stupidest thing I ever did and I don't intend to so much as jaywalk from here on out."

"You robbed a bank," he repeated.

"The man I was living with at the time was the one who waved a gun around and demanded the money—I only silenced the alarm and let him out the back door. That made me just as guilty, of course."

"Why did you do it?"

"Because I was stupid. Over a man." She stood. "That's a mistake I won't make again, either."

"Does Travis know about this?"

"Of course he does. And his parents. I wouldn't ask them to invite me into their home without being honest about my past. I appreciate the chance they're giving me to start over. Their trust really means a lot."

He rose also and stood looming over her—still sexy, but also menacing. She had to force herself to stand firm and not shrink under his cold gaze. "I hope their trust isn't misplaced," he said.

"It isn't," she said, licking her suddenly dry lips.

The lines around his eyes tightened. "Just know, I'm going to be keeping an eye on you," he said.

Delivered in another tone of voice, the words might have been a sexy come-on. But Bette heard only warning behind the words—the words of a cop to a suspect. Though she had achieved her goal of putting emotional distance between herself and Cody, her success left a heaviness in her heart. She supposed part of her had hoped Cody Rankin would be different—able to forgive, even if he couldn't forget.

CODY LAY AWAKE for several hours that night, trying to make sense of that paint can and brush under the sink in the bathroom of Bette's cabin. Surely she would have mentioned finding them there when she pulled out the cleaner and towels to clean the paint off the door.

But she wouldn't have mentioned them if she had known all along the paint was there—known because she had put it there herself, and used it to paint that message. But why? So that he would see it and feel protective?

No—that wasn't her game. She definitely didn't like him hovering too close. And she hadn't put the message there in order to make a fuss with the Walkers—she had refused to mention the incident, and had made him promise not to, either.

But he couldn't assume her motives were those of most law-abiding people, he reminded himself. She had a record. She had admitted to the bank robbery with scarcely a trace of shame. Oh, she had made all the right noises about having learned her lesson and intending to go straight, but how many times had he heard that kind of talk before? Just because she had big blue eyes and a sweet, sincere manner—and a body that made it difficult for him to think straight—didn't mean they shouldn't all be on their guard around her. If she was concocting some scam to cheat his friend or his friend's family, she was going to have Cody to deal with—and he'd make sure her punishment was swift and sure.

On this disturbing thought, he fell asleep, and woke at dawn, stiff and sore. After a hot shower, he walked up to the ranch house, thankful that he didn't run into Bette. He found Travis alone in the dining room, eating breakfast.

"Where is everyone?" Cody asked, helping himself to coffee from a pot on the sideboard.

"We're the early birds," Travis said.

Cody sat, moving gingerly still.

"What's up with you?" Travis asked. "You take a fall or something yesterday?"

"Something like that." Cody changed the subject. "What do you know about your caterer, Bette Fuller?" he asked.

Travis frowned. "Why do you ask?"

"She told me she and Lacy were cellmates—that she served time for bank robbery. She admitted it outright."

"Lacy says she was led astray by her boyfriend, a longtime felon named Edward Rialto."

"Do you believe that?"

"It happens." Travis spread jam on a slice of toast. "And I did check on her—she didn't have so much as a traffic ticket before the robbery."

"She said they caught all but one of the people involved in the robbery," Cody said.

"That's right. The getaway driver evaded capture," Travis said. "Apparently, the car he was driving struck and killed a pedestrian while the gang was fleeing from the bank. He's wanted for vehicular manslaughter as well as bank robbery. The others refused to identify him."

"Including Bette?" Continued loyalty to her "gang" didn't sound good to him.

"She said she had only seen him once, for a few minutes, that they hadn't been introduced and she couldn't identify him."

"Convenient." Cody scooped up a forkful of eggs. "I know I don't have to tell you to be careful, but I'm going to play the role of concerned friend and tell you anyway."

Travis set down his coffee cup and studied Cody. "What's wrong? Has Bette done something, or said something, that's disturbed you?"

Cody thought about mentioning the can of paint and the message on Bette's door, then thought better of it. He had no real proof Bette had put the message there herself, and no motive for her to have done so. Right now, Travis and his parents had accepted having a convicted felon catering the wedding. Cody had no grounds for upsetting them. "No, I just wanted to know more about her. What are you up to this morning?" he asked.

"I'm going to stay here this morning, catching up on paperwork. Gage texted me late last night—he and Dwight made it back to town about two in the morning. I've got two other deputies on duty, and I'll go into the office about noon."

"Do you have other suspects for the murders?"

"Not really." Travis pushed back his empty plate and held his coffee mug in both hands. "There are a few possibilities, but no one who lines up for everyone. The only connection the women have is that they were all in their twenties or thirties, and they all lived here in Eagle Mountain." He pushed back his chair. "There's still a lot to sift through. We'll find him."

"Let me know if there's anything I can do to help."

"Sure. What are your plans for the day?"

"I thought I'd go ice fishing, over on Lake Spooner."

"Sounds good. If you catch enough, maybe we can have a fish fry. There's a bunch of fishing gear in the tack room, if you want to borrow any. I think there's even an ice auger in there." He pushed back his chair. "I'd better get to work. Talk to you later."

AT BREAKFAST HER first morning at the ranch, Bette waited anxiously for Cody to appear. Not that she was looking forward to seeing him again after their tense parting the night before, but since he was the only person who knew about the message that had been painted on the door of her cabin, he was the only one she could confide in now.

This morning, while getting ready for a shower, she had retrieved a towel and washcloth from beneath the bathroom sink and been startled to discover a paintbrush and a can of red paint. She had even cried out, as if she had encountered a snake under there. She was positive the paint hadn't been there earlier, and she wasn't sure what to do about it now. She hated the idea that someone had come into her cabin while she wasn't there, but she didn't know if she should say anything to the Walkers. Cody might not be her friend, but he might have some idea about what she should do.

"Good morning!" Lacy greeted Bette with a hug and walked with her to the breakfast table, where Mr. and Mrs. Walker and Emily were eating.

"Good morning," Mrs. Walker said. "I hope you slept well."

"I was fine," Bette said. No sense revealing she had lain awake for hours, fretting and furious about Cody Rankin. In the cold light of day, it seemed foolish to waste any time thinking about a man like that.

"Glad to hear it." Mrs. Walker smiled. "I know you and Lacy are working on plans for the tea this morning. You're welcome to anything in the house you need in the way of furniture or decorations or ingredients. Just help yourself."

"Thanks," Bette said. "That's very generous."

Mr. Walker checked his watch, then pushed back his chair. "We'd better be going," he said to his wife.

She laid her napkin beside her chair and stood. "We'll see you girls later."

"I have to go, too," Emily said. "I have a conference call."

"I thought you were off school for winter break," Lacy said.

"I am. But research projects don't stop just because school isn't in session. I need to meet by phone with my colleagues about a research grant."

"Emily is an economics graduate student at Colorado State University," Lacy said when she and Bette were alone.

"How is school going for you?" Bette asked as she added cream to her coffee. She recalled her friend had used part of the wrongful conviction settlement money she had received from the state to finance her education.

"I'm only just starting out, but I'm loving it so far," Lacy said. "I'm really looking forward to being a teacher."

Travis joined Bette and Lacy as the women were finishing up their breakfast. Bette had seen pictures of the sheriff before—his efforts to clear Lacy's name, and their subsequent engagement, had made the pages of the Denver paper. But in person he was both more handsome, and more forbidding, than she had imagined. Certainly he welcomed her warmly enough, but it was clear he was tired, and probably distracted by his case.

"You're up early," Lacy said, after the introductions had been exchanged and Travis informed them that he had already had breakfast. "You've been working some long hours lately."

"I'm going to stay around here this morning and catch up on some paperwork," he said. "There are too many interruptions at the office."

"Good idea," Lacy said. "Have you seen Cody this morning? He wasn't at breakfast with everyone else."

"He said something about going ice fishing," Travis said.

Or maybe he's avoiding me, Bette thought. But the marshal didn't strike her as a man who avoided much of anything.

CODY FINISHED HIS breakfast, then collected his coat and his car keys and headed to the tack room. No sign of Doug Whittington stealing a cigarette this morning. He found the fishing gear and selected what he'd need and loaded it into the RAV4 he used as his personal vehicle.

The day was sunny, though bitingly cold, the sky free of clouds and a blindingly bright blue. The road to the lake had been plowed, only a thin layer of snow left in place. Dark evergreens crowded close to the side of the narrow track in a wall that looked almost impenetrable. He passed a pair of cross-country skiers and waved, then turned onto the narrower Forest Service track that led to the lake. This road hadn't seen a plow, but enough traffic to the lake and backcountry ski trails had packed it down so that Cody's RAV4 had little trouble navigating.

Just before he reached the lake, he spotted a silver Hyundai pulled to the side of the road ahead. He passed it slowly. It appeared to be empty, but this was a funny place to park. The snow around the vehicle was churned up, as if several people had been walking around it. He drove on, but something about the vehicle nagged at him, so he decided to go back.

He parked across the road and about fifty yards away from the Hyundai and walked slowly toward it, keeping to the center of the road until he was even with the driver's side door. Then he approached cautiously and peered inside.

A woman stared up at him from the passenger seat, as dead and lifeless as a store mannequin.

Chapter Five

After breakfast, Lacy and Bette moved to the sunroom, just off the main room, to plan the bridesmaids' tea to be held that Saturday. Windows on three sides sent sunlight streaming over plank-wood floors and an overstuffed sofa and two chairs in a faded floral print. Despite the bitter cold outside, the room felt warm and inviting. Bette brought along her planner, menu suggestions, pictures of possible table settings and a notebook for jotting down ideas, and spread these over the massive coffee table.

"You're so organized," Lacy said as she flipped through the pictures of place settings and centerpieces. "I'm very impressed."

"I want to do as professional a job for you as I'd do for anyone," Bette said. "It's very hard to start a new business when you don't have a lot of experience to show. That's why I really appreciate you and Travis giving me this chance."

"I promise to post lots of glowing reviews everywhere—and to recommend you to everyone I know," Lacy said. She put her hand over Bette's. "But I'm not doing this out of the kindness of my heart. I'm doing it because I want a great caterer for my wedding, and I know that's you."

"How do you know?" Bette asked. "The only things I've catered on my own are a couple of birthday parties and a bridal shower. And you weren't there for either one of them."

"But I've eaten your cooking," Lacy said. "And it's wonderful."

Bette couldn't keep back a snort of laughter. "You ate things I cooked in the prison kitchen." Once the warden learned that Bette had culinary training—she had been attending culinary school at night and working weekends for a caterer when she was arrested—he'd seen to it that she was moved to the kitchen. "That's not a great compliment."

"Your food was so much better than anything else they served," Lacy said. "I knew if you could work magic in that setting, you'd be fabulous when let loose on your own."

"I've been doing a lot of practicing since my release," Bette said. She was a good cook, and she had a gift for making occasions special. All she needed was a chance to prove herself—and Lacy and Travis were giving her that chance. She angled one of her notebooks so Lacy could see it. "Here are some menu ideas. If you want a traditional high tea, you'll want scones, with jam and clotted cream, fancy tea sandwiches and a variety of little cakes—maybe petit fours. Those always look so elegant. I could do chocolate-dipped strawberries, if I can get the berries, and there are lots of sandwich choices."

"It all looks wonderful," Lacy said, scanning the lists of dishes and their descriptions.

"How many people will be at the tea?" Bette asked.

"Let's see." Lacy sat back and began counting on her fingers. "There's my mother and Travis's mom, and my maid of honor, Brenda. She's married to one of Travis's deputies, Dwight Prentice. A second marriage, so it was a small ceremony, at Dwight's family's ranch over Thanksgiving. You haven't met her, but she's a dear, dear person."

She held up a fourth finger. "Then there's Maya Renfro—Gage's wife. She kept her maiden name. They had a quick ceremony, too—they ran off to Vegas one weekend without telling anyone. And she'll be bringing her niece, Casey, who is five. Casey is my flower girl, and she's so excited about it. So Casey makes five."

She held up a sixth finger. "Travis's sister, Emily, is one of my bridesmaids, of course." A seventh finger went up. "And last but not least, Paige Riddell. She used to run a bed-and-breakfast here in town, but after it burned down she decided to move to Denver. Her brother and her boyfriend live there—he's a DEA agent. I guess that's all—seven adults, if you include me, and one child."

"A lot of cops in the wedding party," Bette said.

Lacy laughed. "Yes, can you believe it? But I've found out when you hang out with one cop, a lot of his friends are cops, so that becomes part of your life."

"Besides Cody and I assume Gage, who are Travis's groomsmen?" Bette asked.

"There's Ryder Stewart—he's with the state highway patrol. And Nate Hall. He's with Parks and Wildlife."

"A park ranger?" Bette asked.

"Not exactly—a wildlife officer. I guess that's what they call game wardens these days."

So, lots of men with guns who were used to being in charge. "No chance of anyone getting out of line with so many law enforcement officers at the wedding," Bette said.

"When I first got out of prison, it made me nervous to be around so many men in uniform," Lacy said. "But it doesn't bother me now. Travis's friends are all really nice."

"You were innocent and they all know it," Bette said. "They can't look at me the same way."

"Don't say that!" Lacy squeezed Bette's hand again. "Travis was happy to have you here."

"Travis wanted to please you. And maybe, because of his experience with you, he's a little more forgiving than some. Not everyone feels that way." She thought of the cold expression in Cody's eyes last night.

"Has someone said something to upset you?" Lacy asked. "What is it?"

"I told Cody Rankin last night about my record," Bette said. "He wanted to know how I knew you and I figured I might as well come out with the truth. It would be easy enough for him to find out."

"How did he take the news?" Lacy asked.

"About like I expected. He's suspicious, wondering if I'm up to something. He doesn't trust me."

"He doesn't know you," Lacy said.

"I don't care if he doesn't like me," Bette said. "As long as he doesn't hassle me."

Lacy regarded her friend kindly. "I know it can be very hard to start over on the outside when you have a record," she said. "But it will get easier, you'll see. Your business will be a success, and while you might have to tell employers about your conviction, there's nothing that says your new clients ever have to know. In a few years you'll look back on your time behind bars as something awful that happened to someone else."

"Maybe." She picked up her pen. "Now tell me which sandwiches you want for your party, and which of these petit fours and cookies you want to serve. I'd suggest three types of sandwiches, three varieties of cookies and one petit four, or two cookies, strawberries and a petit four, or—"

"Enough!" Lacy held up her hands in surrender. "Too many choices." She scanned the lists again. "Why don't you tell me your favorites and we'll go from there?"

Thirty minutes later, they had a menu plan and a decor scheme. They decided to hold the tea in this sunroom and in addition to tea, they'd have champagne cocktails. The decor would be "winter wonderland," with lots of snowflakes and lace and little fascinators for everyone to wear in their hair in lieu of hats. "This is going to be so much fun," Lacy said.

She left to keep a hair appointment, and Bette headed for the kitchen, to see what ingredients were available, and what she would need to buy. List in hand, she pushed open the door to the kitchen. Rainey leaned against the counter, a cup of coffee in hand, a frown on her face. She straightened when Bette entered. "What do you want?"

"I'm making the refreshments for Lacy's bridesmaids' tea this Saturday." Bette walked to the refrigerator and swung open the door. "I wanted to see what ingredients were already on hand, so I'll know what to buy."

"Don't think you're going to go raiding my kitchen for what you need," Rainey said. "If you need anything, go buy it."

"I can certainly do that." Bette closed the refrigerator. Mrs. Walker had told her to help herself to flour, butter, sugar and anything else she needed, but Bette wasn't going to fight this battle. And she could understand that, if Rainey had purchased supplies with the intent to make certain meals, it could throw a wrench in her plans if Bette came along and used up all the butter in baked goods, for instance. Later today, she'd go into town and shop, and store everything either in her cabin, or in the garage refrigerator.

The back door opened and Doug slouched in. He looked different this morning, a hoodie pulled over his head, shoulders slumped. Rainey stared at him. "What do you think you're doing, coming in here looking like that?" she asked. "You haven't even shaved."

Doug rubbed his chin, the scratchy sound setting Bette's teeth on edge. "I thought I'd grow a beard," he said.

"I won't have one in my kitchen," Rainey said. "They're nasty."

Bette decided she had heard enough and retreated to the living room. She chose a chair by the fire and began to make a long shopping list. She hoped she could find fresh strawberries in Eagle Mountain in January. Real clotted cream was probably out of the question, but she could make her own.

The sound of boot heels on the hardwood floor behind her startled her, and she looked up to see Travis, in full uniform, crossing to the door. So much for sticking around the house to do paperwork.

He noticed her sitting by the fire. "Hello, Bette," he said. "Did Lacy abandon you?"

"She went to get her hair done. But I have plenty to keep me occupied, seeing to the tea this Saturday."

He nodded and slipped into his heavy black leather coat, with a shearling collar. He looked troubled. "Is everything all right?" Bette asked. Maybe he was going into work early because something had happened.

He frowned, as if unsure whether to say anything to her or not. "They've found another body," he said, after a moment. He opened the door. "I have to go."

He left, the door shutting softly behind him. Bette sagged back in her chair and stared at the flames dancing in the woodstove. Another body. Another victim of the Ice Cold Killer. The knowledge made her sick, and a little frozen inside.

Chapter Six

Cody stood with Travis and wildlife officer Nate Harris on the side of the road, as two EMTs carefully removed the woman's body from the Hyundai. Nate, a tall blond native of Eagle Mountain and another of Travis's groomsmen, had been patrolling in the area when the call went out requesting assistance. The men stood hunched against the cold, hands shoved into the pockets of their coats. "I was in this area yesterday and this car wasn't here," Nate said. "In fact, mine were the only tracks on this road then."

"I passed a couple of cross-country skiers on the county road," Cody said. "This road had obviously been driven on—I assumed by other fishermen headed to and from the lake."

"There's better fishing on Lake Monroe," Nate said. "This one doesn't get that much use."

The medical examiner, a portly man dressed in camouflaged snow boots that came almost to his knees, an ankle-length duster and a wool cap with ear flaps, stood to one side, chin tucked to his chest as he watched a crew of EMTs remove the body from the vehicle. Travis had introduced him as Butch Collins, a retired local doctor who filled the role of county medical examiner. When the ambulance doors had shut, Butch moved over to join the three lawmen. "You know, when I took this job, they told me if I had to go out on one call a month for an unattended death, that would be a local record," he said. "This murderer seems determined to keep me busy."

"Any estimate on the time of death?" Travis asked him.

"I'd say she was killed last night," Butch said. "Maybe in the lab I can get a better idea, but she had been there long enough for the tissues to freeze."

"The low was minus nine last night," Nate said.

Butch nodded. "This looks the same as the others to me."

"Hands and feet bound with duct tape, throat slit," Travis said.

"Did you find one of the killer's calling cards?" Cody asked.

Travis took an evidence pouch from his coat pocket and held it so that Cody could see the white, business-card-sized rectangle of cardboard, with the block-print words ICE COLD. "It was tucked in her coat pocket," Travis said, stowing the evidence pouch back into his jacket.

Nate looked up and down the narrow road, snow-shrouded evergreens crowding in close on each side. "Not much traffic out here this time of year," he said. "The road dead-ends at the lake. There aren't any houses or campgrounds along the way. Fishermen use it, sometimes skiers, but no one would be out here after dark in the winter. No reason to be."

"So what was she doing out here?" Cody asked.

"Maybe she wasn't here," Travis said. "Maybe the killer drove her here."

"And walked out?" Cody asked.

"Or was driven out," Nate said. He turned to Travis. "Didn't you tell me once that you think the killer might have an accomplice—or rather, there are two men working to kill together?"

"That seems the most likely scenario to me," Travis said. "Two men working together would have an easier time subduing the women and killing them quickly. Several times the bodies have been found in remote places, which points to someone transporting them there, then leaving in another vehicle."

"Is it twice as hard to find a pair of killers?"

Cody asked. "Or twice as easy? You'd think there would be more evidence with two people. More clues."

"You'd think," Travis said.

"Tell me about the other killings," Cody said. "Were the circumstances of those similar to this?"

"Similar," Travis said. "Kelly Farrow was the first—a local vet. A really vivacious, pretty woman. She had only been in Eagle Mountain four months. A highway patrolman found her car up on Dixon Pass—Ryder Stewart. I think you've met him before. He's in the wedding, too."

"I remembered Ryder," Cody said. "Was the car like this—on the side of the road?"

"It had been buried by an avalanche and Kelly's body was inside. That night, the second woman was killed. Christy O'Brien. She had actually driven the wrecker that pulled Kelly's vehicle out of the snowbank."

"Did the killer know about that connection?"

"I don't know. The third woman, Fiona Winslow, died four days later, on my family's ranch," Travis continued. "We were having a scavenger hunt. She and Ken Rutledge—the man we arrested yesterday—were partnered for the hunt. They had a disagreement and she decided to leave him and join some girlfriends who were hunting as a team. She never made it."

"Rutledge couldn't have killed this woman," Cody said. "Not if he's in jail."

"He's still there," Travis said. "I already double-checked."

"Having someone killed on the ranch hits close to home," Cody said. "Do you think that was intentional?"

"Maybe. Leaving those cards is a way of taunting law enforcement. So would a killing right under my nose, so to speak."

"Who else was at the party?"

"Lots of people. There were a couple of college guys who came to town to rock climb and got trapped by the storm. They knew Emily from school and she invited them out. They were top on my suspect list, but I saw them yesterday at the gas station and they said they were headed back to Denver."

"Worth checking that," Cody said.

"Oh, I will."

Cody studied the draped figure on the gurney. "So this is the fourth victim."

"I was hoping the killer or killers took advantage of the break in the weather and left town," Travis said. "But I guess we couldn't be so lucky."

The license plate on the car had been issued

in Denver—the prefix told Cody that much. "Who was she?" he asked.

Travis consulted a small notebook. "Lauren Grenado," he said. "Her license information has an address in Denver. We found paperwork in the car that seems to indicate she's staying at a condo here in town."

"Is she married? Have kids?" Cody asked.

"The paperwork lists the rental in the name of Adam Grenado. I'm guessing that's her husband. We need to check at the condo and find out."

"I don't envy you that job," Cody said.

"I was hoping you'd come with me," Travis said. "I've called Dwight to stay here and finish processing the scene."

"I'll stay, too," Nate said.

"Then will you come with me?" Travis asked Cody.

Cody didn't hesitate. His friend needed backup, and Cody was more than qualified for the role. "Sure, I'll come."

Travis exchanged a few words with Gage, then signaled that Cody should follow him. They drove around the barriers and headed into town. Travis was on the phone for most of the drive—probably giving instructions to his deputies, and maybe checking in with Lacy. Cody wanted to call his own office, to find out what was going on—what he was missing during his forced time off. But he doubted anyone would tell him anything, and he might have to endure another lecture about how he needed to get his head clear and de-stress. No one seemed to realize how stressful it was to be out of the action so long.

Travis signaled a turn onto a road that skirted town and passed the high school. Three teenagers with snow shovels labored to clear the walkway in front of the school. Travis slowed and rolled down his window. Cody followed suit. "How's it going, boys?" Travis called.

"It's going okay." The tallest of the three spoke, a blond in an expensive down jacket and mirrored sunglasses. The other two boys looked up, their expressions unreadable.

"Keep up the good work," Travis said, and drove away.

Cody parked behind Travis on the street in front of a row of cedar-sided condos, probably purpose-built to rent to summer residents and winter tourists. He joined Travis beside his SUV. "Those boys back at the school," Cody said. "Community service?"

"Yeah. They were involved in a series of pranks that got out of hand. They were near the place where the second murder occurred and I was hoping they might have seen something that could help us, but they say no." He consulted his notebook. "Lauren Grenado was in 2B."

They climbed the stairs to the second floor and knocked on the door labeled B. Beyond the door came the sounds of a television, then someone's approach. The young man who opened the door wore a T-shirt and sweats, his light brown hair uncombed and the shadow of a beard across his jaw. He blinked at them, a little bleary-eyed. "Yes?"

"Adam Grenado?" Travis asked.

"Yeah." He squinted, as if trying to bring them into better focus. "Is something wrong?"

"We need to talk to you for a few minutes. It would be better if we came in."

"Oh, okay. Sure." He opened the door wider and Cody and Travis filed past. Adam rushed forward to sweep a pile of jackets off a chair and pick a blanket up off the floor. The room smelled of stale food. Adam grabbed the remote and muted the television. "What's going on? Is this about Lauren?"

"What about Lauren?" Travis asked. Cody sat back. He saw his role as an observer. He'd let Travis do all the talking.

Adam sank onto the sofa. "She left yesterday," he said. "We had a fight. I guess we got pretty loud. If some of the neighbors complained…" He let the words trail away and shook his head.

"Where was she going?" Travis asked.

"She said she was going out for a drive—that she needed to think."

"You'd had a fight?"

"A disagreement. I wanted to take some money her folks gave us for Christmas and buy a boat, but she didn't think we should do that."

"Where is she now?"

"I don't know. She isn't answering her phone." He picked up a cell phone from the end table beside the sofa and studied the screen. "When she didn't come back last night I tried calling and texting—after a while I'd decided she must have gone back to Denver. She did that to me once before—left me stranded without a vehicle."

"So you haven't been worried about her?"

"A little. But mostly I'm angry. Like I said, she's pulled this kind of thing before—she can be very impulsive."

"What did you do last night when she didn't come back?" Travis asked.

"I got drunk and went to bed." He shrugged. "I'm not proud of it, but that's the truth. Why? What's with all these questions?" The first sign of fear shadowed his eyes. "Is something wrong? Has Lauren been in some kind of accident or something?"

"I'm sorry to have to inform you that your wife is dead, Mr. Grenado."

He stared at them, eyes gone glassy. "No." He shook his head. "No. She can't be dead. She was fine when she left here last night."

"She apparently died last night. Marshal Rankin found her this morning, in her car on a remote Forest Service road." He nodded to Cody.

Adam shook his head. "No. That can't be. How did she die? Was there an accident?"

"No," Travis said. "She was murdered."

The echo of the word hung in the air, stark and ugly.

Adam stared at them a few seconds more, then buried his head in his hands and began to weep, great, racking sobs that shook his body. Travis and Cody waited a moment, then Travis said. "Mr. Grenado, we need you to pull yourself together so you can help us find who did this."

He nodded, and after a visible struggle, sat upright, though his voice broke when he spoke. "Who would do something like this?"

"What did you do after your wife left here last night?" Travis asked. "Did you follow her?"

"No. I stayed here." His eyes widened. "You

don't think I—I would never hurt Lauren. I loved her. Sure, we had had a fight, but we did that sometimes. It didn't mean anything."

"So you were here all night?"

"Yes. I told you."

"Is there anyone who can prove you were here all night?" Travis asked.

"No. I mean, I guess you could ask folks in the other condos if they saw me leave. But I don't have a car. Lauren has it."

"Do you know anyone else who might want to hurt her?" Travis asked. "Have you noticed anyone suspicious hanging around the condo, or following you while you were out?"

"No. Nothing like that. Lauren didn't have any enemies." He scrubbed his hand across his face. "Is this that serial killer? I thought I heard something about a serial killer. Did he kill my wife?"

"What do you know about the serial killer?" Travis asked.

"Not much. We're on vacation, so we haven't been following the news. But we were in a restaurant the other night and someone said something about this guy who had killed three women around here." He frowned. "He had a funny name—you know, how the press always tags these guys with nicknames. Like people would forget them if they didn't have a catchy handle."

"The Ice Cold Killer," Travis said.

"That was it. Did he kill my wife?"

"We don't know, Mr. Grenado," Travis said. "Do you know of any reason your wife would have been out on a deserted Forest Service road last night? Would she have gone there to meet a friend, maybe?"

"No. Lauren didn't know anyone here."

"Why did you come to Eagle Mountain?" Travis asked.

"We wanted a getaway, somewhere in the mountains. And the rates are good this time of year."

"What have you been doing while you're in town?"

"Just, you know—relaxing. We went out to eat. We rented snowmobiles and took them out one day." He shrugged. "We were just hanging out."

"And you didn't see anyone suspicious or encounter anyone who made you nervous?"

"No." His face crumpled again. "What am I going to do?"

"Do you have a family member you can call to come help you?" Travis asked.

He nodded. "My brother. He lives in Denver, but I know he'll come."

Travis stood. "I can send someone from my office to wait with you until he comes."

"No." He rose also. "I'll be okay. Am I supposed to do something else, about my car and about…about Lauren's body?"

"Someone from my office will call you later today with that information." Travis handed him a business card. "If you have any questions, or you think of anything else that might help us, call me."

"Okay. I will."

Travis waited until he and Cody were at the curb again before he spoke. "What do you think?" he asked.

"He's really grieving and logistically, I don't see how he could have done it." Cody glanced around the parking lot. "You'll verify he and his wife only had one vehicle here. And then there's that business card."

"Information about that card has been in the paper."

"So you're thinking this could be a copycat killing?"

"It could be, but I don't think so." Travis looked back toward the building. "I think Lauren Grenado went out alone at night and the killer saw her and took the opportunity to kill her, then drove her to that remote location, thinking it would be a while before anyone found her."

The burden of these killings showed on Travis's face. Cody knew he took each death personally. "I've asked the Colorado Bureau of Investigations to send some help," Travis said. "Now that the road is open, someone should be able to get through."

Cody nodded. "You've been hung out on your own until now. It's a lot for a small department to handle."

"Still, it's my county. There aren't that many people here—I should have been able to handle it."

Cautioning Travis not to be so hard on himself wouldn't do any good. He was wired to take responsibility—it was one of the things that made him a good sheriff. "Tell me what I can do to help," Cody said.

"Right now I need you to go back to the ranch and let everyone there know what's going on. Tell the women especially to be on their guard. They probably shouldn't drive anywhere alone. I already talked to Lacy."

"All right. But if there's anything else, you know I'm here."

Travis stared down the quiet street, snow mounded on the sides of the road, no sign of activity in the surrounding homes. If not for the knowledge of what had happened near here, it would be an idyllic scene of winter peace. "The killer is here, too," Travis said. "And I need to find out where, before he kills again."

Chapter Seven

The town of Eagle Mountain might have been a village in the mountains of Switzerland or Austria—Victorian buildings lining narrow streets in a valley below snowcapped peaks. Glittery snowflake decorations adorned light posts along the town's main streets, and storefronts advertised winter sales. Bette guided her car slowly through town, struck by the jarring discordance of such horrible violence taking place in such a peaceful setting.

It hadn't taken long for news of the latest murder to spread through town. As Bette guided her grocery cart down the aisles of Eagle Mountain Grocery, she overheard customers discussing the murder, speculating on the identity of the latest victim and the motives of the killer. Most people seemed to think the woman who was killed was a visitor to town, since no one knew of any local who was unaccounted for.

Weather and news that the highway remained open were the next most popular topics of conversation, though some people were of the opinion that the town's reprieve wouldn't last. "Those avalanche chutes above the pass are full to bursting and all this sunshine is making them more unstable," one woman said to a friend as they perused the selections in the dairy case. "I'm stocking up while I can, before the snowslides start and they have to close the road again."

Bette selected several pounds of butter and two cartons of cream, then steered her cart toward the center aisles. As she had feared, good strawberries weren't to be had this time of year in the mountains, so she had switched her menu to chocolate-covered dried fruit. She was trying to decide between apricots and cherries when an attractive woman with streaked blond hair approached. "Excuse me, but are you Bette Fuller, the caterer?"

"Yes," Bette said, cautious in spite of the woman's friendliness.

"I'm Brenda Prentice." The woman offered her hand. "I'm Lacy's maid of honor. It's so good to meet you. Lacy has told me so much about you."

How much? Bette wondered. Did Brenda's friendliness mean she didn't know about Bette's past—or that she knew and had decided to give her the benefit of the doubt? Bette hoped it was the latter, but she knew better than to expect that. "It's good to meet you, too," she said, shaking Brenda's hand.

"It was so kind of you to come all this way to cook for the wedding," Brenda said. "I know it means a lot to Lacy."

"I was happy to do it." In her opinion, Lacy was the one who was being kind.

"I'm looking forward to the tea this weekend," Brenda said. "Such a clever idea to do that instead of a girls' night out at a bar."

"It was all Lacy's idea," Bette said. "But it should be a really fun party. Lacy said you're married to one of Travis's deputies."

"That's right. Dwight Prentice. We went to high school together, but it wasn't until after my husband died that we connected again."

"Lacy mentioned you're a newlywed."

"Yes. She still hasn't forgiven me for cheating her out of being a bridesmaid in a big, fancy wedding." She shifted the package of salad she carried to her other hand. "I'd better get back to work. I only swung by to grab something for lunch. See you on Saturday."

"It was good to meet you."

Bette took her time completing her shopping. Brenda had been very nice—exactly the sort of woman she would have pictured as one of Lacy's best friends. If Bette and Lacy hadn't been thrown together in prison, she doubted they would have ever made a connection at all. Lacy came from a conventional family in a small town. She had always been loved and protected and, even after she had been convicted of murder, her family and friends had stood by her.

Bette was a city girl from a broken home. She had been on her own since she was seventeen, and had never had much support from anyone. It didn't take a psychologist to see that was why she had fallen so hard for Eddie. He had not only promised to love and protect her, he had made her believe he couldn't do anything without her by his side. When he told her of his dream of opening a garage, she had believed every word, because she had always wanted to open her own catering business. When he proposed robbing the bank where she worked to get the money to make those dreams come true, she had hesitated only a few hours before he made her believe it was the right thing to do.

She had had years since then to regret her decision, and to see how Eddie had manipulated her. He had never had any intention of opening a garage, and the people he had introduced to her as friends of his who wanted to help had only been criminals like him, out for their share of the take. All Eddie's flattery and lovemaking had been a lie. He had singled her out for attention because she worked at the bank, and he recognized her as someone he could manipulate.

It was a good thing for her the police had caught the robbers. If her arrest hadn't halted her brief criminal career, there was no telling where she would have ended up. Now, thanks to Lacy and people like her, she at least had a chance to live her dream.

She paid for her purchases and loaded them into her car, then drove slowly through town. She had no desire to live in a sleepy place like Eagle Mountain, but she could enjoy visiting here. She hoped she would have the chance to come back in the summer or fall and explore the surrounding mountains more.

Reluctantly, she turned the car and headed back toward the ranch. She didn't look forward to the inevitable confrontation with Rainey when she went to unload the groceries she had purchased. She wasn't anxious to see Cody again, either, though she needed to talk to him about the paint she had found in the bathroom. And she needed to come up with a way to keep intruders out of her cabin.

Her mind full of these thoughts, she didn't

notice the vehicle coming up behind her until it was on her bumper. The dark SUV raced up behind her, the insistent blare of the horn shattering the peace of the quiet countryside. Alarmed, Bette steered her car as far over to the side of the road as she could safely go. The vehicle surged up beside her and she took her foot off the gas, anxious for it to pass. Instead, the car stopped in the road, and the driver got out. She had an impression of black—black pants, black gloves, black coat with the hood pulled up to hide the driver's face. As he raced around the car toward her, she pressed down on the gas, determined to drive away, but the tires spun in the soft snow. The man, whose face she still couldn't see, beat his hands on her closed window. Bette groped for her phone, to call for help. Then the window shattered. A large rock hit the side of her head, then the door opened and the man dragged her out, into the snow.

SNOW HAD STARTED falling again by the time Cody headed back toward the Walker ranch. Flakes whirled toward his windshield in a mesmerizing onslaught and his SUV plowed through already-forming drifts across the road.

So much for his fishing trip. Maybe he'd try again in a day or two, and this time, he'd ask Bette to go with him. It would give him a chance to question her about the paint and about her intentions toward the Walkers, without an audience to overhear.

He didn't see the car on the side of the road until he was almost on it. Snow drifted over the vehicle, which listed in the ditch like a boat taking on water. He braked hard and turned on his wipers in an attempt to clear the snow from his windshield. No movement in the other car, but the vehicle looked familiar. With a jolt, he realized it looked like Bette's Ford.

He punched the button to turn on his emergency flashers and stopped in the road, then bailed out of his RAV4 and trudged down into the ditch and around the car. The driver's side door was open, snow sifting over the upholstery. A large rock rested in the driver's seat. Cody stared at it, trying to make sense of the sight. Fields and woods lined this stretch of road, not rocky cliffs. For that rock to get there, someone must have thrown it.

And where was Bette? Had she gotten her car stuck in the ditch and decided to walk to the ranch for help? But that didn't explain the rock.

"Bette!"

The silence swallowed his shout. He stepped back, intending to set out to look for her. His foot struck something soft and yielding.

Something that groaned.

Bette lay in the ditch, snow sifting over her still body. Cody knelt beside her and felt for a pulse at her neck. Relief flooded him when he found the steady beat and felt the warmth of her skin. "Bette, wake up." He tapped her cheek with the back of his hand.

She groaned and rolled her head away from him.

He pulled out his phone and called 911. "There's been an accident on County Road Seven," he said. "About a mile from the Walking W Ranch. A woman is unconscious."

The dispatcher promised to send an ambulance and a sheriff's deputy. Cody pocketed the phone and examined Bette more closely. Blood oozed from a jagged cut over her left temple, but he could find no other injuries. She groaned again. Cody squeezed her hand. "Bette, it's me, Cody. You're going to be okay."

Her eyes fluttered, snow caught in her lashes. "What happened?" She stared at him, her gaze unfocused, tense with pain.

"I don't know," he said. "I found you here, in the ditch beside your car. You must have been on your way back to the ranch."

She moaned and tried to sit up, but he pressed her gently back down. "The ambulance is on its way," he said. "Don't try to move."

"I'm cold," she said.

Of course she was cold—lying in the snow. Cody stripped off his coat and laid it over her. "The ambulance will be here soon," he said, hoping the words were true.

"What happened?" she asked again.

"Something hit your head. I think a rock. What do you remember?"

She closed her eyes. "I can't remember. I was at the store, talking to a nice woman—Brenda. I bought some butter and cream." She shook her head, wincing. "I can't remember."

"It's okay. Don't worry about it."

"My head hurts."

"I know. It will be all right soon."

She didn't try to talk after that. Had she passed out again? Should he try to wake her? Her hand in his was so cold, a chill he could feel even through his gloves. He gathered her other hand between his palms and chafed them both gently. Her nails were short and she wore no rings—maybe jewelry got in the way of cooking. She had long, slender fingers and delicate wrists. He pressed her palms to his cheek—the skin was like satin and smelled faintly of roses.

She moaned again, and he quickly lowered her hands and tucked them beneath the coat he had draped over her. It didn't feel right, to be studying her this closely while she was unaware. Where was that ambulance?

"Cody?" she asked.

"I'm right here."

"Did you come to arrest me?"

He stiffened. "Arrest you for what?"

"That's what you do, isn't it? You arrest people."

She stared at him, but he had the sense she wasn't really seeing him. "Only if they've broken the law," he said. "Have you broken the law?"

"That doesn't matter, does it?" she said. "You think I'm bad, and I'll never be able to make you believe I'm good." She closed her eyes again.

"Bette?"

She didn't answer, only moaned and shook her head.

The distant wail of the ambulance broke the winter silence. Cody stood and trudged out of the ditch, into the road to flag it down. It parked in the road behind his RAV4 and a middle-aged man and a slightly younger woman climbed out. "Emmett Baxter," the man introduced himself as and shook Cody's hand. "This is Joan Anderson." He indicated the woman, who was taking a large plastic tote from the rear of the ambulance. "What have we got?"

"I'm not sure." Cody led the way around the car. "She's got a head injury."

They knelt in the snow, one on each side of Bette, and opened the medical tote. Cody moved to the bumper of Bette's car, trying to get a sense of what had happened here. He could barely make out the tracks where her car had left the road and gone into the ditch. He wasn't trained in assessing traffic accidents, but he couldn't see any skid marks—no churned earth or deep ruts to indicate she had skidded off the road. Yet surely she wouldn't have deliberately driven into the ditch.

He moved to the front of the car. Except for the broken driver's side window, the vehicle appeared undamaged, though the snow might be hiding some ding or scrape that would tell a different story. Had someone sideswiped her and driven away? Had someone stopped after she had gone into the ditch and, instead of helping her, had thrown the rock through the window and dragged her out of the vehicle? The idea sent a chill through him that had nothing to do with the temperature.

Emmett stood and Cody walked back to join him. Bette was sitting up now, a bandage over the cut on her head. "How are you feeling?" Cody asked.

"I've been better, but I'll live." She looked more alert, though still in pain.

"Do you remember anything more about what happened?" Cody asked.

"No. It's all…just a blank."

"Short-term memory loss isn't uncommon with a head injury," Joan said. "Or with any kind of trauma, really."

"Will my memory come back?" Bette asked.

"Maybe. Maybe not," Joan said. "I wouldn't worry too much unless you start noticing bigger gaps."

"We can take her to the clinic in town, but they can't get her to the hospital," Emmett said. "Dixon Pass is closed again. Chute number nine let loose about half an hour ago. It'll be twenty-four hours, at least, before the road opens. More, if it keeps snowing."

"I want to go to the ranch," Bette said.

"I can take her," Cody said. "There are plenty of people who can look after her there."

"What about my car?" Bette asked.

"We'll get a wrecker, or maybe one of the ranch trucks, to pull it out later," Cody said.

"I'll need my purse and the groceries I bought."

"I'll get them." Emmett moved toward the vehicle, but stopped short when he saw the broken window and the rock. "What happened here?"

He started to reach in for the rock, but Cody caught his arm. "Don't touch anything," he said.

"What, you think someone did this deliberately?" Emmett asked.

"I don't know. But don't touch it. Just get her purse off the passenger seat." He scanned the interior. "The groceries must be in the trunk."

He took the keys from the ignition and pressed the button to unlock the trunk. He and Emmett were retrieving the grocery bags when a black-and-white sheriff's department vehicle parked behind the ambulance and Travis Walker got out. "I heard the call on the scanner, figured I'd better see what was up," he said. He looked over as Bette, leaning on Joan, came around the front of her car. Cody read the relief on his face and realized the sheriff had been worried the victim might be his fiancée, Lacy. "What happened?" Travis asked.

Bette shook her head. "I'm not sure," she said.

"The head injury is hampering her memory of the events," Joan said. She steered Bette over to Cody's vehicle and helped her into the passenger seat.

Travis walked around to the side of Bette's car, where Emmett was packing up the last of the medical supplies. "Looks like someone broke the window with that big rock in the driver's seat," Emmett said. "She must have been sitting in the seat at the time and the rock hit her on the side of the head."

Travis studied the broken window and the rock. "Where is this somebody now?" he asked.

"Bette was the only one here when I showed up," Cody said. "I didn't pass any other cars after I turned on the county road."

"Neither did I," Travis said. "And there aren't any houses between here and the ranch." He looked at Bette again. "She really doesn't remember anything?"

"She says not. It's a pretty nasty gash on the side of her head—she was unconscious when I got here."

"Good thing you showed up when you did," Travis said. "She might have frozen to death before anyone found her."

Cody had been trying not to think of that. "I need to get her to the ranch," he said. "But someone should take a closer look at the car."

"I'll take care of that," Travis said. "The snow is going to make finding tracks almost impossible, but I'll do what I can."

"Thanks."

He returned to the RAV4 and started it up, then turned the heater to high. "You doing okay?" he asked Bette.

"I'll be fine." She stared out the window, not looking at him.

What had she meant, when she had said he thought she was bad? It wasn't true. She made it sound as if he passed judgment on everyone he met, putting them into categories—bad and good. If he did do that, he wouldn't know where she belonged. She had a bad past, and he couldn't say he entirely trusted her, but it wasn't fair for her to say he had made up his mind about her.

When they reached the house, no one else seemed to be around. Cody helped Bette out of the car, his grip firm, yet gentle. "I'll be fine," she said, pulling away from him. "I'll just go to my cabin and lie down for a while." She tried to turn away but almost lost her balance.

"I think you'd better come into the main house for a little while," he said. He put his arm around her. "Let me help. You don't want to fall and bust open your head again."

She gave in and let him help her into the house. He settled her into a chair near the fire. "Thank you for your coat," she said, returning it to him.

He hung the coat on a peg by the door, then returned to sit beside her. "How are you feeling?" he asked.

"I wish people would quit asking me that."

"You'd better get used to it. How are you feeling?"

"I have a pretty bad headache," she admitted.

"Do you remember any more about what happened?" he asked.

"No." Her eyes met his, her expression troubled. "I'm sorry, I can't."

"There's no need to apologize."

"Hello, I didn't hear you come in." Emily came in from the other room, smiling, but her smile vanished when she noticed the bandage on Bette's head. "What happened to you?" she asked.

"I'm not sure." Bette touched the bandage gingerly. "Cody found me on the side of the road, in a ditch."

"Cody! What's going on? Did you call Travis?"

"He's still on the scene. Bette has a head injury—maybe a mild concussion. She can't remember anything. I thought it would be a good idea for her to stay where someone can be with her until we're sure she's okay."

Emily sat beside Bette and took her hand. "You need to see a doctor."

"I called for an ambulance and the paramedics treated her," Cody said. "They couldn't take her to the hospital because an avalanche has closed the pass again."

"I didn't want to go to the hospital, anyway," Bette said. "I'm sure I'll be fine, once I get a little rest. I just wish I could remember what happened. The last thing I remember, I was in the grocery store. I met Brenda—such a nice woman."

"But how did you hit your head?" Emily looked to Cody. "You say you found her in a ditch?"

"Her car was in the ditch and she was lying in the snow beside the car," he said. "The driver's side window was busted out, and a big rock sat in the driver's seat. The rock probably hit her in the head when it went through the window."

"A rock?" Bette stared at him. "But how did it get there? I mean, I always see the road signs that say watch for falling rocks, but I never dreamed one could come through the window like that."

"This wasn't a falling rock," Cody said. "It happened in an area of open fields and woods. There isn't any place near there that a rock could have fallen from."

"Are you saying someone *threw* the rock at her?" Emily asked.

"We don't know," Cody said.

"Who would do something like that?" Emily asked.

He didn't see any point in trying to answer that question. "You might fix her some tea or something," he said. "She was lying in the snow who knows how long and she's probably still chilled."

"I'm sitting right here," Bette said. "If I want tea, I can get it myself."

"I'll get it." Emily stood. "I could use a cup myself."

She left them. Bette glared up at Cody. "Don't you have something to do?" she asked.

"I'm doing it."

"I don't like you hovering over me."

He leaned toward her and lowered his voice. "Want to tell me about the red paint I saw in your bathroom last night?" he asked. He hadn't planned to question her about the paint right now, but why not take advantage of the opportunity?

She gasped. "What were you doing snooping around in my bathroom?"

"I was looking for a towel and I saw the paint and a brush. The same color paint that was used to write that message on your door."

"Why didn't you say something to me about it then?"

"Why didn't you say something to me?"

"Because I didn't know it was there—not until this morning." She clutched at his arm. "I swear that paint wasn't there before last night. Someone—probably the same person who put that message on the door—must have come in while I was out and put it there."

"How did they get in? You locked your door, didn't you?"

"Of course I did, but mine might not be the only key."

"I'll ask the Walkers if there's another key."

"Don't." She drew back. "And don't look at me that way."

"What way?"

"As if you think I'm guilty of something."

"If you're not guilty of something, why don't you want me talking to the Walkers?"

"Because I don't want to worry them over something so stupid. It was just a childish message painted on my door."

"But who wrote it, and why?"

"My guess is someone who doesn't want me here. Someone who wants me to, as the message said, go home."

"I guess Rainey is at the top of that list. And maybe Doug."

"Probably. But it doesn't matter. I'm not going to leave, and there's no sense making a fuss. That's probably what they want. When they realize I'm going to ignore them, they'll have to give up."

"I'd think the Walkers would want to know

if one of their employees is harassing a guest," Cody said.

"They have enough to worry about right now, with the wedding and the snowstorms and the serial killer," Bette said. "I can look after myself. Promise you won't say anything to them."

"All right. I won't say anything."

"Won't say anything about what?" Emily returned, carrying a loaded tray.

Cody stood and relieved her of the tray. He handed one of the steaming mugs on it to Bette and took one for himself. "I asked Cody not to say anything to Rainey and Doug about my injury," Bette said. "I don't want Rainey using it as an excuse to push me out of her kitchen."

"She's bound to hear about it from someone." Emily settled next to Bette with the third mug of tea. "And she's not going to push you out of the kitchen. We won't let her."

"Still, it would be better if you just don't mention me to her," Bette said.

The door opened and Travis came in, followed by Lacy. "Come sit by the fire," Emily said. "The two of you must be frozen."

The couple shed their coats, then Lacy sank into a chair across from Bette. Travis remained standing. "I was on my way home when I saw Travis on the side of the road, with your car,"

Lacy said. "He told me what happened. How are you feeling?"

"I'm fine." She looked up at Travis. "Did you find anything to tell us what happened?"

"Have you remembered anything that happened?" Travis asked.

"I'm sorry, no. I'm trying to remember but…" She shook her head. "I don't even recall leaving the grocery store and getting into my car."

"I'm having your car towed to the station so we can take a better look at it there," Travis said. "If you need to borrow one of the ranch vehicles in the meantime, just ask my mom or dad. They'll be happy to lend you whatever you need."

"I shouldn't need to go anywhere for a few days, at least," Bette said. "I stocked up on supplies today. By the way, I need to bring them inside and put them away."

"I'll take care of that in a minute," Cody said.

"There's something else you should know." Travis took an evidence pouch from the pocket of his coat. "We found this in the ditch near the car."

Bette took the packet from him and frowned at the contents. "Duct tape?"

A chill went through Cody. The Ice Cold Killer had used duct tape to bind the hands and feet of his victims.

"Did you have any duct tape in your car that might have fallen out when you got out?" Travis asked.

"No," Bette said. "It's not something I've ever owned."

He tucked the evidence pouch back into his pocket. "I need to get this over to the station. I just stopped by to see how you were doing."

"I'm going to be fine," Bette said. "Thank you."

"I'll get those groceries out of the car," Cody said. He followed Travis out the door. On the front porch, the two friends stopped. "Did you find any of the killer's calling cards?" he asked.

"No," Travis said. "Just this roll of duct tape. It looks brand-new. I'm not even sure any tape has been used off the roll."

"Maybe the killer ran out and needed more."

"There are only a couple of places in town that stock the stuff," Travis said. "I'll be checking with them." He shoved his hands in his coat pockets. "It's snowing pretty hard, but I got out of the cruiser several times and walked the roadside on the way back to the ranch. I didn't see any signs where a vehicle might have turned off the road—no tracks or depressions in the snow or broken plants or anything."

"Cars don't vanish into thin air," Cody said.

"They don't," Travis agreed. "If whoever attacked Bette didn't turn off and he didn't turn back, that means it came here, to the ranch. And it means he's still here."

Chapter Eight

The idea that Bette's attacker could be here at the ranch put Cody on high alert. "What do you need me to do?" he asked.

"I need you to help me search the ranch," Travis said. "We'll check all the outbuildings and anywhere someone could possibly stash a vehicle."

"Sure. Do you suspect someone at the ranch—an employee or somebody else?"

"Right now, I suspect pretty much everyone."

Cody retrieved Bette's groceries from his RAV4 and stashed them in the garage refrigerator, then he and Travis set out across the ranch.

"If this was the Ice Cold Killer, he's getting pretty reckless," Cody said as he and Travis made their way toward the stables.

"He killed Fiona Winslow in the middle of a party," Travis said. "Anyone could have come upon him at any time. I think that's part of the thrill for him."

"What are we looking for, specifically?" Cody asked, as they stopped behind a trio of vehicles parked near the stables. All three were covered with snow—in one case the vehicle, an older-model sedan, was almost buried in a drift.

"I'm looking for anything that looks like it's been driven in the last two hours," Travis said.

"It's been well over an hour," Cody said. "The engine probably won't be warm."

"No, but we should be able to tell if it isn't covered with snow. We can rule out your car, mine and Lacy's, but anything else we find, we'll take a very close look at the driver."

For the next two hours, they trudged through the snow, knee-deep in places. They peered into sheds and walked up narrow tracks that led into the woods. What few vehicles they spotted had clearly not been moved since the snow started. Travis questioned a few ranch hands, but all denied seeing any strange vehicles—or even any familiar ones. "Not much call to go out in a storm like this," one man said. "Especially with Dixon Pass closed."

By the time they made it back to the house, the sun was setting, and Cody's fingers and toes ached with cold. "Let's check around back here and we'll call it a night," Travis said, leading the way around the side of the house.

"The killer really has nerve if he's stashing

his car this close to the house," Cody said, but he trudged along behind his friend, toward the back door, and the beckoning warmth of the kitchen. They had almost reached that warmth when Travis stopped. "What is it?" Cody asked. He followed his friend's gaze toward the shadows at the edge of the glow from the light shining through the kitchen window. He could just make out the bumper of a car.

He followed Travis over to the car and the sheriff played the beam of his flashlight over the windshield and hood. A scant half inch of snow coated the vehicle, compared with the much thicker coatings they had found on the other ranch vehicles. Travis directed the light to the ground around the car. "Does it look like there's less snow behind the back wheels to you?" he asked.

"That's harder to tell," Cody said. "Maybe. Whose vehicle is this?"

"It belongs to Rainey." He switched off the flashlight. "Let's see what she has to say."

"I'm GOING TO be fine," Bette said, struggling to keep all trace of annoyance out of her voice. Lacy and Emily meant well, fussing over her like two mother hens, but she was beginning to feel a little smothered. They had plied her with tea, ibuprofen, blankets and offers of chicken soup and a hot water bottle, and they didn't want to let her out of their sight, even to go to the bathroom. She pushed aside the blankets and pillows and stood. "I'm going to go check on the groceries Cody put away, and then I'm going out to my cabin. I'm going to take a shower and go to bed early, get a good night's sleep and I'm sure I'll be fine in the morning."

"Shouldn't someone check on you during the night?" Lacy asked. "I mean, aren't you supposed to wake up someone with a head injury periodically, so they don't go into a coma or something?"

"If anyone wakes me up out of a sound sleep I can't be held responsible for the consequences," Bette said.

"You can't blame us for being worried about you," Lacy said.

"I know," Bette said. "And you're being really sweet, but I'll be fine. I'm feeling much better now. I hardly even have a headache." Not exactly true—her head still hurt a lot. But she wasn't going to let on about it or they would insist on taking turns waking her up all night to make sure she didn't die. And if they did that, the only lives that would be at risk would be theirs.

Lacy and Emily exchanged looks. Bette was

sure they were going to argue with her. Before they got the chance, she headed for the kitchen.

Rainey looked up from the pot she was stirring on the stove. "What do you want?" she asked. "I'm in the middle of fixing dinner."

"I don't need anything from you," Bette said. "I'm just going through to the garage."

Once safely in the garage, she switched on the light and pulled open the door to the refrigerator. As she had expected, Cody had shoved both bags full of groceries on top of the cases of beer, not bothering to sort out what required refrigeration and what didn't. Sighing, she pulled out the bags and took out the dried fruit and several other items that didn't need to be kept cold. She would store these in her cabin until she needed them. She wouldn't give Rainey an excuse to complain that Bette's supplies were taking up space in her pantry.

She closed the refrigerator, hooked the bag of groceries to take to her cabin over one wrist and returned to the kitchen—and almost collided with Cody.

He reached out to steady her. "What were you doing in the garage?" he asked.

"I needed some things from the refrigerator." She looked past him, to where Travis stood with Rainey. Neither of them looked happy about something. Travis was scowling and Rainey was hunched, arms folded tightly across her chest.

Rainey glanced at Bette, then looked back to the sheriff. "I always park my car back there," she said. "I don't see what business it is of yours. If your parents have a problem with it, they can tell me themselves."

"I don't care where you park, Rainey," Travis said. "I asked you when the last time you moved the car was."

"Why do you need to know that?" she asked.

"Just answer the question, please."

"Yesterday," she said. "I ran some errands in town and it's been parked there ever since."

"Are you sure?" Travis asked.

"Of course I'm sure," she said. "What is all this about?"

"I noticed there isn't much snow on the car," Travis said. "Not as much as you'd expect if it had been sitting there over twenty-four hours."

Rainey hunched her shoulders more. "Doug cleaned it off for me. I don't like letting snow pile up on it too high. Then it's that much more trouble to clean off. So he swept it off for me."

"When was this?" Travis asked.

"I don't know. Sometime after lunch."

"Where is Doug?" Travis looked around the kitchen. "Shouldn't he be helping you with supper?"

"He wasn't feeling well, so I sent him to his room to lie down. I think he might be coming down with the flu or something."

"I'll need to talk to him," Travis said.

"Why? He hasn't done anything wrong."

"Then there won't be any problem with him answering some questions for me."

"What kind of questions?" Rainey demanded.

"He's a grown man," Travis said. "I think he can speak for himself."

Rainey uncrossed her arms and whirled to face him. "Do you think that badge gives you the right to pick on him?" she shouted. "Just because that woman lied about him in court and he had to go to prison, you think you can blame anything that happens around here on him. When you've invited someone else into your home who is so much worse. You ought to be ashamed of yourself, Travis Walker."

"Rainey." His voice carried a sharp edge of warning.

Bette shrank back, half hiding behind Cody as Rainey turned on her. "She's the one you ought to be questioning," she said, pointing to

Bette. "She robbed a bank, and she's probably planning to rob you all blind as soon as you turn your backs."

Rage fogged Bette's vision. How dare this woman accuse her of wanting to harm people who had been so kind to her. If anyone had dared to say something like that to her in prison, she would have lit into them then and there. Fighting meant losing privileges, maybe even having time added to your sentence. But that was better than losing face. If some of those cons learned they could take advantage of you, they would make your time behind bars a living hell.

This isn't prison, she reminded herself. This was a respectable home, and Bette was here to do a job. She wouldn't let this spiteful woman take that from her. So she held her head up and forced herself to move into the middle of the room. "The sheriff knows I'm happy to answer any questions he has," she said, finding and holding Rainey's gaze. "Now, if you don't mind, I'm going to say good-night. It's been a trying day."

She was halfway across the yard, cold wind freezing the tears that streamed down her face, when Cody caught up with her. "Hey," he said, taking hold of her arm.

"Leave me alone," she said, wrenching away from him.

"I'm going to walk you to your cabin," he said, falling into step beside her.

"I didn't ask you to be my bodyguard," she said.

"No. But someone has threatened you twice in the last two days—and this morning you might have been killed. I'm not going to ignore that, even if you are."

She didn't know what to say to that, so they walked without speaking the rest of the way to her cabin, their footsteps crunching on the snow. "No messages on the door," he said as they climbed the steps to the little porch. "That's good."

"Everything looks fine." She faced him, key in her hand. "All right, you saw me here, you can go now."

"Not until we make sure everything inside is all right." He took the key from her and inserted it into the lock.

She followed him into the room. Everything looked as she had left it. "Everything's fine," she said. *Just—go*, she thought.

But he didn't leave. "I'm sorry about what happened back there, in the kitchen," he said. "But it was all on Rainey. Travis will see that, too. She was upset about him questioning her, so she tried to create a distraction."

Bette sat on the side of the bed. "What was all that about the car?" she asked. "Why was Travis questioning her?"

"We were looking for the car driven by whoever attacked you," he said. "Neither of us passed another vehicle between the turn-off for the country road and your car. If your attacker didn't travel that way, the only other direction he could have gone was toward the ranch. When we looked at cars on the ranch, Rainey's was the only one we found that looked as if it had been cleared of snow in the last few hours."

"Rainey hates me, but forcing me off the road and attacking me with a rock?" Bette shook her head. "She doesn't strike me as the type. She'd rather spit in my soup, or spread rumors behind my back—or announce to everyone that I'm a bank robber and I can't be trusted." That moment in the kitchen when everyone had turned to look at her still stung.

"What about Doug?" Cody asked. "Do you think he was the one who attacked you?"

"I don't know." She curled her hands into fists. "I honestly don't remember anything from the time I was standing in the grocery story with Brenda, until I woke up with you shaking me. It's frightening, having a chunk of your life just missing that way."

"But you can't say Doug wasn't the one who hurt you?"

"No. I guess Doug could have done it, but why?"

"He has a record," Cody said. "He served time for beating up his girlfriend. He put her in the hospital."

"Not exactly a comforting thought, but I can't see why he'd want to hurt me," Bette said. "We haven't said more than half a dozen words to each other since I got here."

"He could have hurt you out of some misguided attempt to protect his mother," Cody said.

"Oh, please!" Bette grabbed a pillow and hugged it to her stomach. "I know Rainey resents my getting to cater the wedding, but it's not like she's out of a job. She's still doing what she's done for years, doing the cooking for the ranch. After the wedding I'll be gone and she'll still be here. That isn't a good reason to physically hurt someone. The petty harassment— sure, maybe she'll make me miserable enough and I'll leave. But violence?" She shook her head. "It's not worth the risk of getting caught."

"Is there someone else who might be a threat to you, then?"

"Who? I know it's a cliché for someone to say she doesn't have enemies, but honestly, I don't."

"What about your ex? The one who talked you into robbing the bank?"

"He's still in prison."

"Do you know that for sure?"

She frowned. When she had first been released, she had been almost obsessive about keeping tabs on Eddie. Lately, that obsession had faded. "The last time I checked was six months ago, but yes, he was still serving his sentence."

"A lot of cons have connections outside prison—people who are loyal to them who will do things for them, like check up on an old girlfriend to make sure she doesn't say something she shouldn't."

"But he's in prison. Nothing I say can hurt him worse," she said.

"There was one member of the gang who was never caught," Cody said.

"So you did check up on me."

His expression remained cool. "Are you really surprised?"

"No. I guess I'd have been more surprised if you hadn't. So yes, the guy who drove the getaway car was never caught."

"You didn't testify against him." A statement, not a question. Oh, yeah, he had gotten all the details, hadn't he?

"I didn't know anything to testify," she said. "I saw him for a few minutes exactly once, and I don't remember anything about him."

"Does your ex know that?"

"Yes. He was the one who made sure I knew as little as possible. He said it was for my protection, but it worked both ways. The less I knew, the less I could testify to."

"All right, so you don't know who the getaway driver is—but he probably knows you. Maybe he's come after you to shut you up."

"That's pretty far-fetched." She held up her hand and began counting off the reasons. "One —how does he know I'm in Eagle Mountain? Two—when did he get here? There was only, what, a two-day window when the pass was open so he could follow me here. And three—and this is the biggest reason I think you're wrong—it's been nine years since that robbery. What are the chances that he's still out there walking around? He probably committed other crimes and is locked up for one of them."

"Maybe he was like you—a dupe for your ex. The near miss scared him into going straight."

"In which case, why would he throw all that away to shut me up?"

"If you identify him, you ruin his life. He

might have a good job now, a wife and a family. Those things are worth taking risks for."

"But this is a crazy risk. And really foolish. Because I don't know anything."

"All right," he said. "But until we find out who's behind these threats, I'm going to be keeping a closer eye on you than you may like."

"Why? Why do you even care?"

"Let's just say it gives me something to do. I can only take so much shoveling snow and chopping firewood."

"What are you doing here at the ranch anyway?" she asked.

"I'm one of the groomsmen."

"Yeah, but the wedding is two weeks away. Why are you here so early?"

He studied her for a long moment, silent.

"It's a simple question," she said.

"But it doesn't have a simple answer." He stared at the floor, then let out a long, slow breath. "I told you before I'm on vacation, but that's just the polite word for it. Actually, it was more of a forced leave."

"What happened?" she asked. "Did you screw up? Shoot someone you shouldn't have?"

He winced, and she wanted to take the words back. "I'm sorry," she said. "I shouldn't have assumed."

"It's okay. I'd rather you said what you were

thinking than try to tiptoe around my feelings. I've had enough of that."

She waited for him to say more. The silence stretched, until she became aware of the gentle sigh of his breath and the brush of the denim of his jeans when he shifted in the chair. "I was on a job," he said finally, his voice low and tight, as if he was forcing out the words. "Routine stuff—pursuing a fugitive with a warrant. The guy was wanted for sexually molesting his ten-year-old niece. Nice, upstanding citizen— a banker. A girls' soccer coach, so there was a question of whether other girls were involved. Basically, I thought he was scum, but I would never have let him know that. I did my job— tracked him down at a friend's cabin where he had gone in a pretty feeble attempt to hide from the cops. I gave him my usual spiel of how he should come with me quietly."

He closed his eyes, and she sensed he was replaying the scene in his head. "He had a gun. He was waving it around. One of those cases you hate, because the way he was holding the gun, I could tell he wasn't really going to shoot me. He was trying to commit what we call suicide by cop. But I wasn't going to let that happen."

He opened his eyes again. "It's a matter of pride for me that when I go after someone, I bring them back alive ninety-nine percent of the time. I knew I could handle this guy. I wasn't in a hurry. I had all the time in a world to talk him off the ledge, get him to put the gun down. There are rules for handling these kinds of things and I knew how to follow them to reach a good outcome."

He fell silent again, the lines around his eyes so deep, the hunch of his shoulders that of a man in pain. "What happened?" she whispered.

He licked his lips. "He didn't know the rules. I was right that he didn't want to shoot me. Instead, he shot himself. Put the barrel of the gun in his mouth and pulled the trigger. He was looking me right in the eye when he did it."

She put a hand to her mouth to stifle the cry she couldn't keep back.

Cody shook his head, like a boxer shaking off a blow to the chin. "It rattles you, something like that. But I knew I could deal. I told my boss the best thing for it was to get back out in the field, but he didn't see it that way. He ordered me to take time off—to get out in nature, to see a counselor if I needed. But not to come back on the job until February."

"So you came here."

"I couldn't just sit around my apartment. And Travis is a great guy for giving you perspective. You might not see it, but the man is beyond calm in a crisis. I figured he and I could hang out, go fishing, I could work on the ranch. But he's tied up chasing a killer, and I'm going crazy." His eyes met hers again. "That's where you come in."

"So I'm going to be your distraction."

"Oh, you're a distraction all right."

He stood and moved toward her. There was nothing subtle about his stance, or the look in his eye. She felt that look like a bottle rocket straight to the middle of her chest, the heat of the explosion radiating down through her middle to pool between her legs. Something pulsed between them, and her gaze shifted from the almost painful fire in his eyes to his lips, the bottom one a little fuller than the upper, the black shadow of whiskers above the upper lip.

He took the pillow from her and tossed it aside, then pulled her up to face him, one hand at her waist, the other beside her left breast as his lips crushed hers. She returned the fierceness of that caress, kissing him as if her next breath depended on it, opening her mouth and tangling her tongue with his, wanting—insisting—on having all of him, right this minute.

It was a long time before he dragged his head up, breaking contact and staring into her eyes with a look that was equal parts desperation and defiance. "If you want me to leave now,

I'll go," he said, his voice a rough growl that scraped across her nerves. "But you'd better be sure it's what you want."

"What do you want?" she asked. It wasn't a question so much as a dare.

"I think you know that." His lips closed over hers again and she surged up, her whole body bowing toward him, her hands clutching his biceps, fingers digging into his taut muscles. He grasped her hips and ground against her, leaving no doubt of his desire.

Her need for him thrilled and frightened her. Some small voice in the back of her mind said she was being too reckless. It was too soon. She hardly knew this man. He—

She told the voice to shut up and grabbed the hem of the fleece pullover he wore and shoved it upward. Then they were tearing at each other's clothes with an urgency that would have destroyed less sturdy garments.

She pulled him down to the bed on top of her, then he rolled until she was straddling him. She laughed at the heady feeling. "What's so funny?" he asked.

"Haven't you ever laughed simply because something felt so good?" she asked.

"I don't know. If I ever did, it's been a while."

"Then I'll have to see if I can change that." She slid down his body and took him in her mouth, surprising a gasp from him. He caressed and kneaded her shoulders as her mouth worked on him, then he dragged her back up to meet his mouth with hers. "Let's not end this too soon," he said, with some effort. His gaze searched hers. "Are you sure you're up to this? I forgot you had a pretty hard blow to the head."

"I read an article once that said sex was better than painkillers for getting rid of a headache," she said.

The slow, sexy smile he gave her could have melted chocolate. "Then I'll do my best to make you forget the pain," he said. It was his turn to surprise her, as his skillful fingers delved and fondled. When he began licking first one breast, then another, she squirmed against him. "Do you like that?" he asked.

"No, I hate it. Can't you tell?"

In answer, he drew the tip of one breast into his mouth, while his fingers moved more deftly.

Her climax rocketed through her, fierce and freeing. She collapsed against him and he held her—rather tenderly, she thought, which made her blink back foolish tears. She propped herself up on her elbows and met his gaze. "It's, um, been a while," she said, almost sheepishly.

"I'm a very lucky man," he said. He flipped her over on her back and moved between her legs.

She grasped his shoulder. "Wait."

His eyes met hers, and she saw the moment he recognized the problem. "We don't have any protection," he said.

"Hmm. Then we'll have to work around that."

She started to slide down the bed, but he pressed her back against the pillows. "Wait a minute," he said, and got up.

He disappeared into the bathroom and returned seconds later, a gold foil packet held aloft. "Where did that come from?" she asked.

"The medicine cabinets in these cabins are fully stocked," he said. "The Walkers think of everything for their guests' comfort."

"I didn't see those before," she said.

"You weren't looking." He parted her knees and knelt between them. "I was."

She wanted to ask him what he meant by that but was distracted by the sight of him sheathing himself. And then he was moving into her, and she didn't want to think about anything for a while. She only wanted to lose herself in the sensation of being filled and surrounded and uplifted by this man.

Such a wonderful feeling.

And a dangerous one. But she didn't want to think about the danger now. She'd have all kinds of time for thinking later.

Chapter Nine

Bette untangled herself from the bedcovers the next morning, aching in body and mind. Her head hurt and her muscles ached, but worse than that, her emotions felt bruised. Cody had stayed long into the night, making love with such tenderness and ferocity, before slipping away some time very early this morning. What was it about him that made her want to be so reckless? He had given her probably the best night of her life, but this morning she was no more certain about where she stood with him than she had been at this time yesterday.

She dressed and emerged from the cabin into a world frosted in white. Sunlight sparkled on the drifts of snow that covered everything, transforming woodpiles and old machinery into glittering confections. The air was so sharp and clean it hurt to breathe. She felt energized with every inhalation. She found Emily, Lacy, Travis and Cody in the dining room, digging into an egg-and-ham casserole that smelled mouth-watering. "How are you feeling this morning?" Lacy asked. "Does your head hurt?"

"Only a little. I feel fine." A little beat up, perhaps, emotionally and physically, though for long moments last night she had forgotten all about her headache, or anything else. But all the closeness and compatibility that had come so naturally last night in the intimacy of her cabin felt a lot shakier and out of reach here in the real world. She poured coffee, avoiding looking at Cody, though she was as aware of him as if he were the only person in the room.

"I'm so glad," Lacy said. "I had to make myself not go out there in the middle of the night, just to make sure you were okay."

Bette was glad she had her back to the table as she served herself from the buffet. Her cheeks burned with the memory of what Lacy might have found if she had decided to visit the cabin last night. "I'm glad you restrained yourself," she said. "I was fine." Though *fine* was a poor word to describe what she had been feeling last night—*elated*, *transported*, even *awed* would have been better choices.

"I have something fun for all of us to look forward to," Emily said. "Gage and I have decided we should have an old-fashioned sleigh ride to take advantage of the snow. Dad agreed we could use the old sleighs that are in the barn—he and Mom are out there now, checking the harness."

"When did you and Gage decide this?" Travis asked.

"Yesterday. He telephoned the ranch, wanting to talk to you, but you were in the kitchen with Rainey, so he and I got to talking. Casey has been begging to go on a sleigh ride ever since he showed her that album of family pictures that Mom gave him. We figured with all this snow, now is the perfect time."

"When is the sleigh ride?" Travis asked.

"Tonight, after supper," Emily said. "We'll hook up both sleighs and ride over to the little line shack in the south pasture. We can have hot chocolate and maybe s'mores." She nudged him. "Don't look so stern—it will only be for a few hours, and it will be a nice break from all the tension. We've all been feeling it, you know—not just you."

"It sounds like fun," Lacy said. "Romantic."

"Very romantic," Emily agreed. "We'll have lots of fur robes and blankets for snuggling under, and Gage promised to bring a flask of peppermint schnapps for spiking the hot cocoa."

"That sounds like Gage," Travis said drily.

"Oh, you're going to enjoy it," Emily said.

"I wouldn't dream of disobeying orders." Travis kept a straight face, but Bette didn't miss the sly look he sent Lacy across the table.

Lacy sat up straighter, her cheeks only slightly pink. "It does sound like lots of fun. I'll be looking forward to it. In the meantime, I have a Skype meeting with the wedding planner this morning." She looked around the table. "What are the rest of you doing today?"

"I'm working here for a while, then heading to the office," Travis said.

Cody made no comment, eyes focused on his plate. Bette had the strong impression he was pretending not to have heard Lacy's question—when, really, he didn't want to answer it. "I'm a little concerned about how a couple of my recipes will turn out at this altitude," she said. "I thought I'd make some test batches, in case I need to tweak things."

"I've talked to Rainey," Travis said. "She shouldn't give you any trouble."

"Thank you." Bette settled in the chair across from the sheriff. He really had been so kind to her—Lacy was lucky to have found a man who was so perfect for her. "If they turn out well, we can use them for more refreshments for tonight."

"Any idea when the road might reopen?" Cody asked.

Travis shook his head. "They'll be working this morning to clear the avalanche chutes."

"What does that involve, exactly?" Bette asked.

"They use dynamite, or sometimes a grenade launcher, to explode the snow out of the chutes and create a slide—an intentional avalanche," Travis said. "All the snow ends up on the highway and they have to haul it off. There are twenty-four chutes in that section of highway, so clearing them can take several days. And there's more snow in the forecast."

"Why don't they build another road?" Bette asked. "It's crazy to have a whole town full of people who can't go anywhere every time it snows."

"The road usually only closes for a few hours, maybe half a day, at a time," Lacy said. "Some winters it doesn't close at all. This winter is just particularly bad."

"There's nowhere to put another road," Travis said. "Not without spending hundreds of millions of dollars to blast through mountains. And it would probably be subject to avalanches, too. The people here are used to it. They know how to cope." He slid back his chair and stood. "I need to get to work."

The rest of them finished breakfast and left the table one by one, until Bette was the only person left. She lingered over coffee, wanting to give Rainey time to finish the dishes and clear out. She wasn't afraid to confront the cook, but it would be easier on everyone if she didn't have to.

About ten o'clock, she retrieved the ingredients she needed from her cabin and returned to the kitchen, relieved to find it empty. She pinned up her hair, then slipped her apron over her head, some of the tension draining from her body as she did so. She smiled to herself as she began assembling the tools and ingredients she needed. This was the best therapy. So many times, when her life had felt out of control, she had found solace in the kitchen. Mixing, kneading, stirring, basting—here she was ruler of her own domain, a magician who had the power to conjure beautiful things from simple ingredients.

She went into the garage to get the cream and butter she needed for the tea cakes. She found the butter immediately, but where was the cream? She moved items around and even looked to see if somehow the carton had slipped behind the cases of beer. But the cream simply wasn't there. She shut the door, confused. Had the cream been left behind when Cody transferred the groceries from her car to his? No—

she was sure it had been there last night when she rearranged everything.

She returned to the kitchen and began opening doors and searching everywhere for the missing cream. She was being silly—there was no reason the carton would have ended up anywhere in these cabinets. But she couldn't shake the compulsion to look.

And then she found it, sitting on a middle shelf in the kitchen's walk-in pantry, next to a jar of roasted peppers. The carton was warm in her hand, and before she even opened it, she knew it would be spoiled. Disgusted, she dumped the contents in the sink, rinsed the carton and tossed it in the recycling bin. She knew she hadn't put the cream in the pantry, which meant someone else had—probably Rainey or Doug.

A shadow passed in front of the window. She looked out and spotted Doug, shoulders hunched, hood pulled over his head. She grabbed a coat from a peg by the back door and shoved her feet into a pair of women's snow boots—no doubt Rainey's. Let her complain about Bette borrowing her coat and boots and she'd get more than an earful in return.

She found Doug huddled next to a tall stack of split firewood, cupping his hand around a cigarette to light it. "Doug!" she called.

He jumped and almost dropped his cigarette. "What do you want?" he asked, half turning away from her.

"Someone took a quart of cream from the garage refrigerator and put it in the pantry to spoil," she said. "Did you or your mother do that?"

He blew out a stream of smoke, which hung in the cold air between them. "You probably did it yourself. I heard you got hit in the head. It probably made you loopy."

She took a step closer; he moved a step back. "What do you know about that? Did you hit me in the head?"

"Why would I do that? I never laid eyes on you before you showed up here."

"So why do you and your mother hate me?" The answer to that question was behind all this, wasn't it? "It's not like I'm trying to take your jobs," she continued. "I'm just catering the wedding of a friend. Then I'm going to go back to Denver and you'll probably never see me again."

"You should just go back now." He flicked ash into the snow.

"You're the one who painted that message on my door, aren't you?" she asked.

"I don't know what you're talking about. I

just think it would be a lot less trouble for everyone if you went home now."

"Since the pass is closed, that's impossible. But why do you care if I'm here or not?"

"Who said I cared?" He dropped the cigarette on the snow and ground it out with the heel of his boot. "If you've got a beef with my mom, take it up with her."

"I'll do that. Where is she?"

"She went to her room to lie down. Said she had a migraine. You won't get anywhere talking to her right now." He left, moving along the edge of the woodpile and staying as far from her as possible, keeping his head down.

Bette stared after him. What was up with this guy? He wouldn't even look at her.

She returned to the kitchen and shed the coat and boots. She'd make do without the cream today and go into town tomorrow to buy more. For the moment, she would leave Rainey alone. She wouldn't get anywhere if the woman really did have a migraine. Instead, she would focus on baking, and getting ready for the bridesmaids' tea. Those were things she could control, in a world where so much was out of her hands.

CODY WALKED BY the kitchen, refusing to give in to the temptation to go in and talk to Bette.

He could hear her in there, opening and closing doors, rattling bowls and pots. He imagined her, focused on her work, the scents of vanilla and cinnamon clinging to her, mingling with her own sweet essence, the memory of which made him hard.

He hadn't gone to her cabin last night intending to take her to bed, but he wasn't sorry he had. She got to him. He hadn't talked to anyone about what had happened on his last assignment—not even the shrink his bosses had made him see—before last night. He had been certain that he didn't need to talk about it. Talking didn't do anything but pull the scab off the wound.

But telling Bette had been easy somehow Once he had made up his mind to talk to her, he had *wanted* her to know. He didn't feel the need for barriers with her. He couldn't say that about many other people. Last night had been powerful, but he wasn't sure what it meant for the future.

Hell, he didn't know if he even had a future. He might as well admit that, if only to himself. He didn't know if he would have a job waiting for him when he reported back to the US Marshals Service in February. He had heard rumors of budget cuts and restructuring for months now. An officer they saw as "damaged" would be first in line to be let go.

He needed to work—to prove he could still do the only job he had ever really wanted. With this in mind, he knocked on the door of Travis's home office, half of a suite of rooms he occupied on the ground floor, just off the kitchen. "Come in," the sheriff called.

Dressed in his sheriff's department uniform, as if at any minute he might be called out, Travis sat behind a scarred wooden desk in a small, cluttered room that resembled, in many ways, the cramped space he had claimed at the sheriff's department in Eagle Mountain. Cody stepped in and closed the door behind him and Travis looked up from a laptop computer, but said nothing.

"What can I do to help?" Cody asked.

Travis pushed the laptop to one side. "Aren't you supposed to be on leave?" he asked. Cody had told his friend some—but not all—of what had happened.

"I'm not an invalid," Cody said. "I need something to do and you need help. Deputize me or something." He sank into a cowhide-covered armchair across from the desk. "Besides, with the pass closed, you're not going to be able to call in help from the state. I'm the best you've got."

"Then I'd better not turn down your offer," Travis said.

"So what can I do? Is there someone you want me to interview? Something you need researched?"

"You've spent more time with Bette than I have—what's your feel for her?"

Cody had an immediate, intense image of heated, satiny skin sliding beneath his fingers. He kept his face stony, betraying nothing, hoping Travis wouldn't notice how tightly he gripped the arms of the chair. "What do you mean?" he asked.

"Is she really reformed?"

"She seems serious about her catering duties, and I haven't found any evidence of wrongdoing." He didn't see any need to mention his suspicions about the painted message on her door. As evidence of a crime, it was pretty weak, especially since she'd refused to say anything about it to the Walkers.

"There's a *but* at the end of that sentence," Travis said. "But what?"

"But she has a record. And bank robbery is a pretty serious crime." He couldn't forget that, no matter what else he thought about her.

Travis nodded.

"Why are you asking me about her?" Cody

asked. "Do you know something about her I don't?"

Travis sat back, hands clasped over his stomach. "Have you considered the possibility that no one attacked her?"

"What do you mean? Someone threw that rock and hit her in the head."

"She could have driven the car into the ditch, then gotten out, picked up the rock and thrown it through the window herself. We didn't find any blood in the car."

Cody frowned. What Travis described was certainly possible. "Why go to all that trouble?" he asked. "And it doesn't explain the head injury."

"We only have her word for it that it was a bad enough injury to cause memory loss," Travis said. "The EMTs weren't able to x-ray her, or perform any other tests. The cut didn't require stitches. Maybe she bashed her own head."

Would Bette do something like that? Then again, was it any more far-fetched than his suspicions that she had painted those words on her door? Some sick people worked to call attention to themselves, even if it meant hurting themselves. "Again—why?" he asked.

"I don't know." Travis frowned. "I'm not saying that's what happened. I'm just trying to look at all the possibilities."

"Then why not focus on the most likely scenario—that she was attacked by the Ice Cold Killer and something scared him off?"

"What scared him off?" Travis asked.

"Maybe my arrival."

"You didn't see a car. We never found a car or any sign of one."

"Did you talk to Doug Whittington?" Cody asked. "He could have driven his mother's car."

"I talked to him," Travis said. "He said he was sleeping in his room all afternoon. His mother vouches for him."

"I think Rainey would lie to protect her son," Cody said.

"Maybe. But I can't find anyone who remembers the car not being parked near the kitchen yesterday, or anyone who saw Doug in Rainey's car. Rainey's story about having him brush the snow off her vehicle so it wouldn't pile up is plausible."

"Then maybe it was someone else," Cody said. "There was a big time gap between when I found Bette and when we started looking for a vehicle. Time enough for someone to hide a vehicle where we couldn't find it. And we were hampered by the snow. This Ice Cold Killer has done a good job of eluding detection so far."

"This doesn't fit the pattern of his other victims," Travis said. "They were subdued and bound fairly quickly, especially in the case of Fiona Winslow. Yet he didn't even have time to get any tape off the roll we found. And the whole deal with the broken window and the rock—it's sloppy. It doesn't feel like the same man."

"Maybe he felt rushed. Maybe he's getting desperate."

"There are too many *maybes* with this case."

"What do you think we should do?" Cody asked.

"Nothing right now. But keep your eyes open. Let me know if you notice anything suspicious."

"I will." He didn't need an excuse to watch Bette closer, but Travis had just given him a reason to take the job even more seriously.

Chapter Ten

"Oh, it's lovely weather," Lacy sang as she stepped out onto the front porch, arm in arm with Travis.

"For a sleigh ride together with you!" Bette joined in. The sleighs stood ready in the drive—old-fashioned wagon boxes with curved sides, painted bright red and hung with silver bells that glinted in the light from the lanterns hung at the four corners of the sleighs. The horses—two teams comprising four big draft horses hitched to each sleigh, their manes and tails combed and braided—stood between the shafts of the sleighs, their harness also hung with bells, which rang out with every shake of their heads or stamp of their hooves.

"Right this way." Gage, a red scarf wound around his neck above the collar of his shearling jacket, ushered the group toward the sleighs. "Find a seat on one of the benches in the sleighs," he instructed. "There are plenty of blankets for keeping warm, and a few buffalo robes, too."

Bette hopped up onto the wooden crate that served as a step into the sleigh. Someone reached up to steady her and she glanced back to see Cody, his hand at her back. "Where did you come from?" she asked. She had looked for him when she had first stepped onto the porch and hadn't seen him anywhere.

"I'm sticking close." He joined her in the sleigh and took her arm to pull her to the bench at the very back.

She opened her mouth to protest that she didn't necessarily want to ride next to him, but who was she kidding? The thought of snuggling under a buffalo robe with this man made the prospect of this evening even more pleasant. He slid in next to her and pulled the heavy covering over them. Bette sank her gloved fingers into the thick, black fur of the robe, smiling at the sensation of softness and warmth.

"You're in a good mood tonight," Cody said.

"Baking always puts me in a good mood," she said.

"All kinds of lines come to mind about cooking something up with you," he said. "But for now, I'll resist."

"You'd better." But she took his hand underneath the robe.

"More coming aboard!" Gage declared, and assisted a petite young woman, the tips of her dark hair dyed a bright blue, into the sleigh, followed by a little girl dressed all in pink, from the pom-pom of the knit hat pulled over her blond braids to the toes of her snow boots.

"That must be Gage's wife, Maya, and her niece, Casey," Bette whispered to Cody.

"I think you're right," he said.

The little girl's fingers flew, and Bette realized she was using sign language. Gage responded in kind, and said, "I've got a seat saved for us right up front so you can see the horses." He settled her on the front bench between himself and Maya, and tucked a blanket securely around her.

In addition to Gage and his family, Bette's sleigh contained Mr. and Mrs. Walker. Lacy and Travis rode with Dwight and Brenda Prentice and Emily in the sleigh ahead of them. Though only a few days ago the presence of so many law enforcement officers would have made Bette uncomfortable, she was more at ease with them now. She could even admit their presence tonight made her feel a little more secure.

A ranch hand, swathed in a long leather duster, climbed aboard to take the reins of their sleigh. "Giddy up!" he called, and with a jolt, they surged forward, then glided smoothly over the snow. Casey laughed and clapped her hands and Bette felt like joining in. There was something magical about floating over the snow on a cold night, the stars overhead like diamond dust, so bright and sharp that if she reached up she feared she might cut herself.

"There you go, smiling again." Cody leaned close and spoke in a low voice. "Makes me suspect you're up to something."

"I'm always up to something." She watched him out of the corner of her eye. "I thought you knew that."

He let go of her hand, but only to slide along her hip, his fingers coming to rest between her thighs. "So am I," he said.

She looked away, lifting her face to the rush of icy air across her cheeks, aware of the strong beat of her pulse in time to the jingle of the sleigh bells, of the skitter of sensation across her skin as Cody languidly rubbed his thumb up and down the seam of her jeans. For so many years in prison she had kept herself numb, pretending feelings like these didn't exist. If you didn't let yourself feel, then you couldn't hurt. Pretending that avoiding emotion made her stronger was a habit she had carried into life after she was freed. How quickly Cody had proved that belief to be a lie!

"Oh, it's lovely weather!" Emily sang out, and the others joined in to sing "Sleigh Ride"— slightly off key, but with great gusto. Cody's voice, a tuneful baritone, mingled with Bette's clear alto, and she thought how well they sounded together.

Almost too soon, the sleighs stopped before a flat-roofed log cabin, the windows outlined with white lights. A cowboy came out to meet them, and everyone piled out of the sleighs and trooped into the cabin, which glowed with the warmth of a wood fire and half a dozen lit oil lamps.

Two cowboys passed out tin cups, then came around the room with kettles of hot chocolate and ladled the hot drink into the cups. Another man served platters of the tea cakes and cream puffs Bette had made that afternoon.

The young woman with the blue hair approached with the little girl. "I'm Maya," she said, offering a hand. "And this is Casey."

Casey held out one of the cream puffs and signed with her free hand. "She says she really likes the cream puff," Maya said. "I told her you made them."

"I did." Bette smiled at the little girl. "Tell her I'm glad she likes them."

"And you must be Cody." Maya turned to the man beside Bette. "Gage has told me about you and I know you've been staying at the ranch, I just haven't made it up there since you arrived."

"I'm pleased to meet the woman who could put up with Gage," Cody said.

"Don't say that." Gage joined them. "I'm the underdog in my own house now. These two team up on me all the time."

"Excuse me if I don't feel sorry for you," Cody said, grinning at Maya.

"That's a beautiful ring," Bette said, nodding to the silver band on the third finger of Maya's left hand. "May I see?"

Maya held out her hand. The filigree band sparkled with brilliant pink and blue stones. "I wanted sometime simple, so Gage had it made. All the materials are from Colorado. The stones are Colorado rhodochrosite and aquamarine."

"It's gorgeous," Bette said.

"You should see the rings Travis and Lacy picked out," Maya said. "Gage and I went with them to pick them up."

"Sometimes my brother has good taste," Gage said. "Or maybe I should say Lacy has good taste."

"If you're saying something about me, it had better be good," Lacy said, as she pushed in between Gage and Cody, Travis right behind her.

"I was just telling them about your wedding rings," Maya said. "How beautiful they are."

"I'm really happy with them." Lacy looked at Travis. "You should show them to them when we get back to the ranch house."

Travis's brow furrowed. "Isn't that bad luck?" he asked. "To see the rings before the wedding?"

"That's the wedding gown," Lacy said. "And I want them to see them."

"All right," Travis said.

Emily joined them. "Everyone having a good time?" she asked.

"We are," Bette said. "This was a great idea."

"It was mine," Gage said.

Emily punched him. "It was not. It was mine."

"It was your idea to have a party," he said. "I suggested the sleighs."

"All right, I guess I'll give you that."

His expression sobered. "It's good to have a night off…from everything else."

A shiver ran up Bette's spine. For a little while, she had forgotten about the killer who was preying on women in the area. She imagined the thought of him seldom left Gage's and Travis's minds.

Maya slipped her arm into Gage's. "No work talk," she said. "We agreed."

"That's right." He raised his arms over his head and began clapping. Everyone turned to look at him. "Finish up the snacks, people," he said. "Part two of the evening's festivities are about to begin."

"What are we going to do now?" Bette asked, handing her cup to the man who came to collect it.

"Party games," Emily said. "You have your choice of cornhole or bowling." She held up a small beanbag and a plastic bowling pin.

Groans rose from around the room. "Don't be sticks in the mud," Emily said. "This will be fun." She began dividing them into teams. Bette found herself assigned as one of the cornhole players. The object was to pitch a small beanbag into a hole on a slanted board set up at the other end of the room. Cody was nowhere to be seen. *Coward*, she thought, as she hurled her first beanbag toward the game board, only to have it land in the floor only halfway to the target.

"I'm horrible at this!" she complained a few minutes later, after her third miss in a row. She gladly relinquished her beanbag to the next person in line and looked around for some avenue of escape.

Cody had emerged from hiding. He grabbed her hand and pulled her toward the door, where he helped her into her coat and slipped on his own. "Where are we going?" she asked.

"Just to get some fresh air." He glanced back toward the game players. "Unless you're dying for another turn at cornhole."

"No!" She zipped up the coat and slipped her hands into her gloves.

Outside, the first blast of icy air made her catch her breath and made her wonder at the wisdom of being out here. But when Cody set off around the side of the cabin, she hurried to catch up with his long strides. "Where are we going?" she asked. "It's freezing."

"I brought you out here to get warmed up."

"Cody, that sentence doesn't even make sense."

"Oh, no?" He pulled her to him and lowered his lips to hers.

She returned the kiss, slipping her arms inside his open coat and around his back. She loved that he was taller than her, but not too tall—exactly the right height for kissing. "Are you warm yet?" he asked, smiling down at her.

"I don't know." She wiggled against him. "Maybe you should try again."

He kissed her again, and she willingly lost herself in the bliss of that moment, floating on a mix of desire and contentment and anticipation.

A burst of noise several minutes later made them jump apart. Cody glanced over her shoulder toward the front of the cabin, where light spilled onto the snow from the open front door. "I think everyone's getting ready to leave," he said.

"I guess we'd better go with them," she said.

"Or we could let them leave behind us and spend the night here by ourselves," he said.

"Right. But I didn't see a bed in that cabin, did you?" she said. "And the few chairs I spotted didn't look that comfortable."

"Home it is, then."

They loaded into the sleigh and Cody put his arm around Bette as they settled onto the back bench. She leaned her head on his shoulder and closed her eyes, half drowsing in his warmth and the magic of the moment. She wanted to sear times like this in her memory, stamping them over recollections of darker times in her life, when such bliss had seemed utterly unreachable—happiness so far from her grasp she couldn't even fantasize about it. Her life was so different now, and she never wanted to take even one moment for granted.

Back at the ranch house, everyone gathered in the great room, saying their goodbyes. "Don't go yet," Lacy said. "I promised to show you the rings. Travis, would you get them right quick?"

The sheriff headed out of the room and Lacy turned back to her guests. "We found this jeweler in Cheyenne who does these incredible Western designs—mostly belt buckles and things like that, but he does wedding rings, too. We had them made from the gold from melting down my grandmother's wedding ring and rings from both Travis's grandparents."

Travis rejoined them, but empty-handed. His face wore a pinched expression. "What's wrong?" Lacy clutched his arm. "Where are the rings?"

"I had them in the top drawer of my dresser," he said. "They're gone."

TRAVIS'S ANNOUNCEMENT SHIFTED the mood in the room. Everyone fell silent, looking at each other. Cody looked, too, examining the faces of those around him. Did anyone seem unsurprised by this news? Did anyone look guilty?

Lacy, white-faced but trying to maintain her composure, clutched Travis's arm. "Maybe they fell behind the dresser," she said. "Or you accidentally put them in another drawer."

Travis shook his head. "They were there this morning when I got dressed. Now they're gone."

"You mean someone came in and stole them?" Travis's mother stared at her son.

"I don't know, Mom," he said. "I don't know what else could have happened."

"It couldn't have been any of us," Maya said. "We were all together at the sleigh ride."

"It might have happened earlier today," Travis said. "The last time I saw the rings was this morning."

"This house is full of cops," Emily said. "You ought to be able to figure out who did it." She turned to the others. "In the meantime, the rest of you should go on home. Thank you for coming."

She and Lacy helped usher people out the door. Maya took Casey and Brenda with her, and Gage promised to catch a ride home later with Dwight. Then the law enforcement contingent—Travis, Gage, Dwight and Cody—gathered in a corner of the room. "I think you can rule out family," Dwight said. "Your mother and father and Emily, and, of course, Lacy wouldn't have any reason to take the rings."

"Maya and Brenda only came to the sleigh ride," Gage said. "They're out."

"All the employees have been with the family a long time," Travis said. "I'm not saying one of them didn't do it, but I can't think why."

"Doug Whittington hasn't been here that long, has he?" Cody asked.

"He has a record," Dwight said. "Though not for theft."

"There's someone else here who has a record," Gage said. "For robbery."

A chill ran through Cody. "I don't think Bette—"

"You don't know she wouldn't," Gage said. "None of us really know much about her. And she was working in the kitchen all day—right next to Travis's rooms."

Cody nodded. Gage was right. He couldn't let his personal feelings for Bette cloud the fact that on paper, at least, she looked like the ideal suspect. "How do you want to handle this?" he asked.

"I'll talk to Doug first," Travis said. "I think just you and me. He knows both of us, so that may put him more at ease."

"Do you want Dwight and me to talk to Bette?" Gage asked.

"Wait," Travis said. "Let's see what we hear from Doug first."

They found Doug and Rainey in the kitchen, washing cups and plates brought over from th cabin. Rainey turned when Travis and Cody er tered the kitchen, but Doug remained hunched over the sink. "What can I do for you two?" she asked.

"We wanted to talk to Doug for a bit," Travis said. He crossed the room and opened the back door. "It won't take long."

Rainey dried her hands and started to remove her apron. "Just Doug," Cody said, and looked hard at the young man. It was a look that had induced many a suspect to be more cooperative, and it worked on Doug, as well. The young man tossed his dish towel on the drain board and followed Travis out the door, Cody close behind.

Outside, the cold bit through Cody's fleece pullover and jeans, and he noticed Doug was already shivering. Maybe that was part of Travis's plan. Instead of sweating the truth out of Doug, he planned to freeze it out of him. "What do you want?" Doug asked.

"Have you been in my room today?" Travis asked.

Doug blinked. "Your room? You mean your bedroom? Here?"

"Yes. Have you been there?"

Doug shook his head. "No. I never go in that part of the house. I mean, why would I?"

"Have you seen a couple of rings I had in there?" Travis continued. "Gold wedding rings."

"No. I told you, I don't go in there. I keep to the kitchen and the dining room and my room. Mom was real clear about that when I moved here."

"Have you seen anyone else in or near Travis's room?" Cody asked.

"Is something missing?" Doug asked. "Is that why you're asking all these questions?"

"Have you seen anyone near Travis's room?" Cody asked again.

He hesitated, then said. "I think I saw that Bette woman. Not in your room, but in the hall just outside of it."

He was lying. Everything in his manner—the shifting eyes, the defensive hunch of the shoulders, as if he was expecting a blow, told Cody his words were a lie. Did Travis see it?

"What time was this?" Travis asked.

"I don't know. This afternoon. She was supposed to be in the kitchen, baking. Mom had told me to stay out of her way. So I thought it was strange she was in the hall in that part of the house."

"Where were you when you saw her?" Cody asked.

Another long pause. "I was just, you know, crossing the great room. I thought I might have left my gloves in there."

"Why would you have left your gloves in there if you never go in there?" Cody asked.

Doug flushed. "I didn't say I never go in there."

"Thank you, Doug. You can go back in now."

The young man left them. As soon as the door closed behind him, Cody turned to Travis. "He's lying," he said.

"Maybe." Travis turned and walked around the side of the house.

"Where are you going?" Cody asked, hurrying after him.

"Let's talk to Bette."

The light over the door to her cabin was lit, and Bette opened the door within seconds of Travis's knock. She was very pale, her lips in a tight line, and she wouldn't meet Cody's gaze. "Come in," she said. "I've been expecting you."

The two men filed in. Bette sat on the edge of the bed—just as she had last night. Cody took the same chair he had used last night, too, while Travis remained standing. "We're asking everyone what they know about the missing rings," the sheriff began.

"You asked Doug," she said. "Now you're asking me. That's not everyone. Just the people with prison records."

Travis didn't react to this accusation. "Do you know anything about the missing rings?" he asked.

"No. I'm not a thief. The bank job—that was one time. And it was stupid. Something I'll regret the rest of my life. But it doesn't matter to you how many times I say I'm sorry, does it? People like you are going to blame me for the rest of my life." Her voice broke on the last words, and Cody had to curl his fingers into his palms to keep from reaching for her. He pushed away the emotion here, freezing it out. Bette wasn't his lover right now—she was a suspect.

"Someone said they saw you near my room this afternoon," Travis said.

"Who said that?" she asked. "Rainey or Doug? They both hate me. They'd say anything to get me into trouble."

"Why do they hate you?" Travis said. "You didn't know them before you came here, did you?"

"No," she said. "Lacy said Rainey was upset that she wasn't chosen to cater the wedding, so maybe this is all part of that resentment. Some people are like that, building grudges into rage."

"I've known Rainey a long time," Travis said. "She gets upset at people, but she's not a liar."

Bette said nothing, merely stared at him.

"Were you in my room at any time today?" Travis asked.

"No," she said. "I've never been in your room. And I didn't take the rings. I didn't even know about the rings."

"Lacy didn't mention them to you when the

two of you were talking about the wedding?" he asked.

"No," she said. "I mean, I assumed there would be rings, but we never discussed them."

"Beyond their monetary value, they have a great deal of sentimental value," Travis said. "Especially to Lacy."

"I know. But I didn't take them. I wouldn't do something like that. I would certainly never hurt the person who is my best friend in the world."

"Do you know anyone else who might have taken them?" Travis asked. "Have you seen anyone suspicious in the house?"

"No. I'm sorry, I don't."

Travis glanced around the cabin. "Do you mind if we take a look?"

"You want to search my cabin?" She stood, face flushed, eyes bright with tears. "You mistrust me that much?" This last question was directed at Cody.

"You don't have to submit to a search," Cody said. "But doing so is the quickest way to establish your innocence."

"Oh, sure, because you couldn't just believe me or anything simple like that." She threw up her hands. "Go ahead. Rifle through my belongings. You won't find a ring."

The look she gave him made Cody feel black

inside. Whatever the two of them might have started last night, it had ended now. He turned away, to Travis. "Where do you want to start?"

Chapter Eleven

They found the rings in Bette's cosmetic case, the box wrapped in a piece of tissue and stuffed beneath tubes of lipstick, mascara and eyeliner. When Travis showed it to her, she went so white Cody poised to catch her, thinking she might faint.

She shook her head. "No." She covered her mouth but couldn't hold back a sob. "I swear on my mother's grave, I don't know how that got there." She looked at Cody. "You believe me, don't you?"

His throat hurt as he tried to get the words out that she needed to hear—that yes, he believed her. Of course he knew she wouldn't take the rings.

But he had spent years training to believe what was right before his eyes. He dealt daily in evidence and rules of law based on hard facts, not emotions. So, though his heart wanted him to say the words, it couldn't overrule his head.

Travis slipped the ring box into his pocket. "Are you going to arrest me?" Bette asked.

"As long as the pass is closed, you can't go anywhere," Travis said. "I don't want to upset Lacy, so for now we'll leave this, while I investigate further."

She sank to the bed again, face buried in her hands. As Cody followed Travis out of the cabin, her sobs hit him like blows. He didn't even feel the cold as they walked toward the house, but when Travis stopped on the porch and turned to him, Cody said, "If that was the right thing to do, why do I feel so awful?"

"Do you think she took the rings?" Travis asked.

"It doesn't matter what I think," Cody said. "We have a witness who said he saw her outside your room this afternoon, and we have the rings in her possession."

"And we have her record."

"Yeah. And we have her record."

Travis pulled out the ring box and looked at it. "I don't think she was faking her shock when we found the ring box."

"Maybe she thought she'd hidden it too well," Cody said.

"It was a lousy hiding place," Travis said. "And she could have put up more of a fuss about us searching. She's been in the system, so she knows her rights. She could have insisted we get a warrant. But she didn't."

"She's right that Doug and Rainey resent her," Cody said.

He nodded. "But if she didn't take the rings, how did someone get into her room?"

"Is there more than one key to those cabins?"

"Yes. There are at least two—maybe three," Travis said.

"Do a lot of people know where they're kept?"

"They're in my dad's office," Travis said. "But it isn't locked. Anyone could get in there."

"This isn't the first time someone may have been in Bette's cabin while she wasn't there," Cody said.

"Oh?"

Cody glanced at the cabin door. "Can we go inside to discuss this? I'm freezing out here."

Travis blinked. Cody thought his friend probably hadn't even noticed the cold until now. "Sure. We'll go into my office."

"Travis!" Lacy called from her seat by the fire when he and Cody entered. He waved her off and led the way across the room to his office.

Cody sank into the cowhide-covered chair and let the warmth of the room wash over him. Travis sat behind the desk. "Bette thinks some-

one has been in her cabin before?" he asked.
"Why didn't she say anything to me or my parents or Lacy about this? How do you know about it?"

"She didn't want to upset your family," Cody said. "She felt they had enough to worry about, what with the upcoming wedding and a serial killer running around. Also, I think she didn't want to call attention to herself or get any kind of reputation as a complainer or a troublemaker. She didn't tell me that, but that's the impression I get."

"That answers part of my question," Travis said. "When did someone go into Bette's cabin, and how do you know about it and I don't?"

"It happened the first night she was here," Cody said. "I walked her to her cabin—mine is the one next to hers. Someone had painted the words *Go Home* in red paint on her door. She washed it off before anyone else could see, and she made me promise not to tell anyone."

"That's still outside her cabin," Travis said. "You said someone was inside."

"I'm getting to that," he said. "The next night I walked her back again, and this time, I went inside. While I was there, I used the bathroom, and when I opened the cabinet to get a towel to dry my hands, I saw a can of red paint and a brush there."

Travis waited, a skeptical look on his face. "I didn't say anything about it to her," Cody said. "I even played with the idea that Bette had painted the door herself, but I couldn't figure out why she would do something like that. If it was a ploy to call attention to herself, it failed, because I was the only one who saw."

He shifted in the chair. "Later—after her accident, when we were talking—I asked her about it and she said she hadn't seen the can of paint in the cabinet until she was getting ready to take a shower the next morning. She thinks someone was in her cabin while she was out— someone who had a key."

Travis considered this. "So that same someone could have taken the rings and planted them in Bette's cabin, knowing she would be a suspect in the theft, because of her past."

"Right," Cody said. "Except who would do that, and why? Would Doug and Rainey really go to so much trouble to get rid of her? Would they take such personal risk just so they could cater your wedding? It doesn't make sense."

"No. Is there anyone else who might want to get rid of Bette?"

"Whoever attacked her on the road," Cody said.

"If that's the case, her attacker wasn't the Ice Cold Killer," Travis said.

"Did your investigation of Lauren Grenado's murder turn up any new evidence?" Cody asked, grateful for a momentary shift of focus.

"Nothing so far." Travis sat back, the chair creaking underneath his weight. "The business cards are generic cardstock available at pretty much any office supply or craft store and online. The printer is a laser printer—we don't have the expertise to determine a particular brand. The duct tape, again, is a brand that is sold by the millions in hardware stores and home improvement centers. We checked with the stores here in town that sell it, but their records haven't turned up anyone suspicious making a purchase. We've turned up some hairs and fibers from the vehicles, but we're still waiting on test results from the ones we were able to get to the lab before the road closed. No fingerprints. No DNA. No other physical evidence to speak of."

"Is this killer that skilled, or just that lucky?" Cody asked.

"Maybe both," Travis said. "I'm still hanging on to my theory that we're looking for two people, not one. The speed of the crimes points to that. It takes time to subdue and secure a conscious victim and, except for Fiona, the evidence points to the women being conscious until they're killed. Fiona was hit on the head with a rock, but that may be because it was the most public of the killings, and therefore necessitated silencing her immediately."

"And no suspects?" Cody asked.

"There are always suspects," Travis said. "I have a couple I want to interview again tomorrow, if you want to come with me."

"Yes." Cody sat up straighter. He had been dying to have more of a role in the case.

"I'd be interested in getting your perspective on these guys," Travis said.

"What are you going to do about Bette?" Cody asked.

"You two are friends," Travis said. "Talk to her. Feel her out on this theory that someone planted the ring. See if she can come up with possibilities."

"I'll talk to her," Cody said. Though he doubted the friendship they had been building could ever be repaired after tonight. She thought he had betrayed her.

Part of him thought that, too.

"I THINK IT would be better if I didn't cater your wedding," Bette said to Lacy as she pulled her aside after breakfast the next morning. She had lain awake half the night agonizing over what she should do. Travis was willing to let her walk around free for now, but his accusations had cast a pall over what was supposed to be a happy occasion.

"What are you talking about?" Lacy stared at her, confusion filling her hazel eyes.

"After what happened last night, I don't think it would be right for me to have a role in the wedding." Bette twisted her hands together, determined to remain businesslike and not upset her friend more than she had to. "Travis doesn't trust me and I would never, ever want to come between you two."

"What are you talking about, silly?" Lacy took Bette's hand and pulled her down onto the sofa beside her. The two were alone in the great room. "What makes you think Travis doesn't trust you?"

"He thinks I stole your wedding rings."

Lacy's eyes widened. "He does not!" Lacy put her arm around her friend. "He found the rings last night," she said. "He'd misplaced them, that's all."

Bette couldn't look at her friend. Travis must have told Lacy that lie to protect her. He certainly hadn't done it to save Bette.

"I don't want anyone else catering my wedding," Lacy said. "Besides, you've worked so hard already. Those cream puffs and tea cakes you made yesterday were divine, by the way. I know people don't come to weddings for the food, but my guests are going to be blown away by your dishes. Besides, where do you think I'd get a caterer this close to the wedding?"

"Rainey and Doug could do it."

Lacy snorted. "Please! If I wanted to serve steak and potatoes and apple pie, they'd do a fine job. But I don't want that."

"Travis would probably like it," Bette said.

"He'd love it. But he'll like your food, too. He's not as hidebound as he comes across sometimes."

Last night in her cabin, the sheriff had been as unbending as steel. Obviously, Lacy knew another side of him.

"Come on," Lacy said, patting Bette's back. "You need to get away from the ranch for a while. Let's go to town and poke around in some of the cute shops and have lunch."

"All right," Bette said. "While we're there, I need to stop by the store and get some more cream."

"Didn't you just buy some?" Lacy asked. Before Bette could reply, she laughed. "I probably shouldn't have eaten so many of those cream puffs last night—cream puffs, indeed. They'll probably go straight to my hips. Let me get my purse and we'll go right now. I'll meet you by the car."

Bette trudged through the snow to her cabin,

torn over what to do next. She had thought to spare her friend pain by resigning from the catering job and quietly fading away. She could find some place in town to stay until the pass opened again. She would have to let Travis know her new address, of course. Otherwise, he might think she was trying to leave town to escape charges.

Was he going to press charges? Should she try to find a lawyer to represent her? The idea dragged at her like a lead coat. She had thought she was past ever having to deal with lawyers and courts and prison again. Yet here she was, being sucked right back into that life. Maybe the real reason so many people returned to prison wasn't that they went back to a life of crime, but because everyone around them assumed they were guilty whenever anything bad happened.

She tried to push these worries aside and focus on having a good time with Lacy. As her friend drove, she chattered happily about the upcoming bridesmaids' tea, the wedding, honeymoon plans and all the things that should capture a bride's attention. Bette listened and nodded and faked enthusiasm. Whatever happened, she was determined it wouldn't spoil Lacy's happiness. She believed Travis wanted that, too, which meant he would do what he could to avoid making a big scene. For now, she would try to be thankful for that small consideration.

Eagle Mountain, with its beautiful setting and access to hiking, skiing, Jeeping and other outdoor activities, catered to tourists. The town's main street was lined with shops selling everything from antiques to climbing equipment to T-shirts. Bette and Lacy spent the morning admiring the clothing in the boutiques and the decorative items in gift shops. Bette even purchased a ceramic chicken designed to hold a recipe card or ingredients list in its beak. She hoped after she left here the item would remind her of her friend—and not the sad way they had parted.

As they headed into the Cake Walk Café for lunch, Lacy hugged Bette. "I'm so glad you could be here for my wedding," she said. "You are one of the dearest people in the world to me. I don't know if I would have survived those years in prison without you."

Bette returned the hug, struggling for composure. "You would have survived," she said. "You're a lot tougher than you look."

Inside, they took a table by the window, looking out onto the town's main street. Tall berms of snow formed a wall on each side of the pavement, and long icicles hung from the eaves, the sun highlighting intricate ice crystals. Under happier circumstances, the effect would have been magical.

After they had ordered, Bette said, "I always knew you were innocent of the charges against you."

"How did you know?" Lacy asked.

"The man who died—your boss?"

"Andy Stenson."

"He was stabbed, right?"

Lacy nodded.

"I couldn't see you doing that—ever," Bette said. "You're just not that type. You don't have a hair-trigger temper. You don't get frustrated easily. If you didn't like your boss, you would quit and find another job. You wouldn't kill him."

"No, I wouldn't."

Bette picked up the paper cover from the straw in her glass and began tying it in knots. "I don't mean to bring up a painful subject," she said. "But what Travis did to you—accusing you of murder and sending you to prison— it was so awful."

"Yes."

"You used to talk about how much you hated him. And now it's easy to see how much you love him. What happened to change that?"

Lacy traced a line of condensation down the

side of her water glass with one finger. "I guess I learned to see past my anger to Travis himself," she said. "To the kind of man he really is. He arrested me not because he disliked me personally, but because he believed at the time that it was the right thing to do. A man had been killed and he believed the man's family—his widow, Brenda—deserved justice. That's not just an abstract term to Travis. He really believes in it. Which is why, when he found evidence that proved I was innocent, he did everything in his power to see that I was released, and the real killer apprehended."

The tender expression on Lacy's face when she spoke of her fiancé made Bette feel teary again. Or maybe that was just her general state of mind today. She touched her friend's hand. "You're a very lucky woman."

Lacy nodded. "I am."

Bette frowned. "Did you say the murdered man's widow was Brenda? Is that Dwight's wife?"

Lacy nodded. "Brenda Prentice was Brenda Stenson. It's kind of crazy, all the connections. But that's part of life in a small town."

"And she never held her husband's death against you?" Bette asked.

"I don't think so." Lacy squeezed her hand. "Forgiveness is a really powerful thing."

After lunch, they headed to the grocery store to buy the cream Bette needed. As they headed up an aisle from the dairy section toward the cash registers, they had to squeeze past a tall gray-haired man, his shoulders hunched. He turned to look at them and Bette gasped and stepped back.

The man grinned. "Hello, Bette," he said. "Somebody told me you were here in town. Small world, isn't it?"

Bette grabbed Lacy's hand and pulled her toward the cash register. She all but threw her money at the startled clerk and hurried out of the store.

Lacy caught up with her in the parking lot. "What was all that about?" she asked, a little breathless.

"Let's just go." Bette tugged at the handle of the locked passenger door on Lacy's car.

"All right." Lacy unlocked the car and slid into the driver's seat.

Bette leaned back against the seat, trying to control her breathing. She watched the exit of the store to see if the man followed them out, but he did not.

"Who was that back there in the store?" Lacy asked as she turned onto Main Street. "Why did he frighten you?"

"I knew him as Carl. Just Carl. No last

name." She shook her head. "He was a friend of Eddie's. He was one of the bank robbers."

"Oh," Lacy said, the one syllable full of understanding. "What is he doing in Eagle Mountain?"

"I don't know."

Lacy pulled the car to the curb and stopped. "I guess I understand why seeing him would have been a surprise, but why are you so terrified? I mean, you're trembling."

Bette clenched her hands in her lap. "I guess I—he was a really good friend of Eddie's. I thought, maybe Eddie sent him after me."

"Why would Eddie do that?" Lacy asked.

"Eddie threatened to kill me if I told the police anything about the robbery and any of the people in it," Bette said. "Of course, I testified at my trial about what I knew. Everyone but the getaway driver had already been arrested and the police had more than enough evidence to convict them. Nothing I said added to that. But Eddie might not have seen it that way."

Lacy turned off the car and unbuckled her seat belt. "We need to tell Travis this right away," she said. "That man may be the one who attacked you the other day."

Bette looked over and realized they were parked in front of the sheriff's department. The last person she wanted to see right now was Travis Walker. But Lacy was right. Carl might be the key to the whole crazy mess she was in.

Chapter Twelve

"Tell me about these guys we're going to talk to," Cody said as he rode with Travis toward town. All the coffee he'd drunk at breakfast in an attempt to be more alert after a sleepless night had left him wired and jittery. He welcomed this expedition to interview two suspects as a distraction from thoughts of Bette.

"Alex Woodruff and Tim Dawson," Travis said. "They're undergraduates at Colorado State University, where Emily is doing her graduate studies. She knows them casually. Their story is that they came up here to ice climb and got stranded when the road closed earlier this month. They're staying at a vacation cabin that belongs to Tim's aunt."

"Does their story check out?" Cody asked.

"I didn't have any luck getting in touch with the aunt, but the cabin is registered to her. They are students and they do climb."

"Why are they suspects in the murders?" Cody asked.

"They can't account for their whereabouts when the first two women—Kelly Farrow and Christy O'Brien—were killed. They were at the ranch the day Fiona Winslow died. I want to ask them what they were up to the night Lauren Grenado was murdered."

"There are two of them and you think two men are responsible for the murders," Cody said.

"I don't have enough evidence to get a warrant to search their property, or to request hair and DNA samples to look for a match to what we've got," Travis said. "All I can do is keep a close eye on them."

The cabin where the students were staying was outside town, on a snow-packed Forest Service road. When Travis pulled up to the square log building with a rusting metal roof, it was clear the driveway hadn't been plowed since the last storm. The windows of the house were dark and no vehicle sat under the attached carport. "Looks like no one's been home in a while," Cody said.

"Let's take a look."

Crossing to the house meant post-holing through thigh-deep snow. Cody followed Travis, instinctively taking up position behind and to the right of him, one hand on his Glock. The house might look deserted, but someone inside could be watching their approach, ready to ambush them when they got closer.

But no gunfire or other noise greeted them as they stepped onto the porch. The shades were drawn over the windows and the door locked. Cody looked around. Snow had settled and crusted over the firewood pile and an old bucket that sat overturned near the carport. "I don't think anything here has been disturbed in a while," he said.

"They must have gone back to Fort Collins when the road opened up." Travis turned away and headed back toward his SUV. "I'll contact the university and the police in Fort Collins and double-check with them."

Back in the SUV, Travis put the vehicle in gear and turned back toward town. "Depending on when they left town, they couldn't have killed Lauren Grenado," he said.

"That place looks like it's been empty more than a couple of days," Cody said.

Travis nodded. "On one hand, it's good to rule out innocent men."

"On the other, it bites not having a good suspect for the murders," Cody said.

"I need to stop by the office, if you don't mind hanging out there awhile," Travis said.

"No problem." Cody stretched. "I'm desperate enough for work I'll even fill out reports for you."

As they approached the sheriff's department, Travis said, "That looks like Lacy's car parked out front."

"What did she say when you told her about the rings?" Cody asked.

"I didn't." Travis sighed. "I knew it would upset her terribly if I told her about Bette, so I pretended I had found the rings in another drawer. I don't like to lie to her, but I couldn't think what else to do."

"You don't know that Bette took the rings."

"I don't. And maybe because of what happened with Lacy—that wrongful conviction—I'm more inclined than most to give a person the benefit of the doubt. There are a lot of things about what happened last night that don't quite fit."

He drove around behind the station and parked, then he and Cody entered through a back door. Adelaide met them in the hallway. "Sheriff, Lacy and—"

"Thanks, Addy. I saw Lacy's car out front. I assume she's in my office." He moved past the older woman. Cody nodded to Adelaide, and followed Travis into his office.

He stopped short when he saw not only Lacy,

but Bette, seated in front of Travis's desk. Both women looked upset about something.

Travis moved behind his desk. "Close the door," he said to Cody, then turned to Lacy. "What's wrong? Has something happened?"

Lacy looked to Bette. She pressed her lips together, as if debating whether to speak, then said, "I saw a man in the grocery store just now—one of the other bank robbers. It…it frightened me. I don't know why he's here."

"What this man's name?" Travis asked.

"Carl. I just know him as Carl."

Travis turned to his laptop. As he typed, Cody watched Bette, willing her to look at him. But she kept her head down, staring at her clasped hands in her lap.

"Carl Wayland," Travis said after a moment. "He was released from the Englewood Federal Correctional Facility six months ago. This was his second conviction for armed robbery, and he has a record of a few other lesser crimes— auto theft, one count of menacing. He took a plea bargain in the bank robbery case, thus the lighter sentence."

"What is he doing in Eagle Mountain?" Lacy asked.

"What do you think, Bette?" Travis asked.

Bette shook her head. "I don't know."

"Did he recognize you also?" Travis asked. "How did he behave?"

"Oh, he recognized me. He smiled and said someone had told him I was here." She looked ill. "I don't know, it just struck me as if…as if he had been looking for me."

"Do you think he's the person who attacked you on the road?" Cody asked.

"I don't know. I still can't remember anything about that attack."

"Did he say anything else?" Travis asked. "How long he's been in town, where he was staying—anything?"

"No. I didn't give him a chance to say anything else. I just left."

"Have you been in touch with him, or with anyone else who was part of that robbery, at any time since your release?" Travis asked.

"No! I don't want anything to do with any of them."

"Have any of them tried to contact you? Any phone calls? Letters? Other encounters?"

"No. Never."

Travis angled the computer toward the women to show a mug shot of a man in his fifties with thinning gray hair and a wispy gray goatee. "Does he still look like this?" he asked.

"Yes," they chorused.

"He was wearing a black leather jacket," Lacy said. "And jeans."

Travis swiveled the computer back around. "I'll find him and try to learn what he's doing here."

Lacy took Bette's hand. "Come on," she said. "Let's go back to the ranch. Travis will take care of this now."

Bette rose and the two women left the office. When they were gone, Travis looked up from the laptop again. "What do you think?" he asked Cody.

"I think Bette is terrified of this man. And I think she's telling the truth."

"I think so, too." He stood. "Come on. Let's go see if we can find Carl."

"He's not going to admit it if he is after Bette."

"No. But we might be able to warn him off. A con with a record like his might think twice about going after a woman who's under the protection of a couple of cops."

"I like the way you think." He followed Travis back outside, the image of Bette's terrified white face haunting him. In all the time they had been in the office together, she had never once looked at him. It was as if he no longer existed for her. That hurt worse than if she had stabbed him in the heart.

WHEN BETTE AND Lacy returned from town, Lacy insisted on going over the seating list for the wedding reception, as well as reviewing the menu for both the reception and the bridesmaids' tea. Bette knew her friend was trying to distract her from her worries, and she was grateful for the attempt, but nothing could make her forget for long the shock of seeing Carl standing in the aisle in the grocery store in Eagle Mountain.

What was he doing here, unless he had somehow followed her? A man like Carl wouldn't have any business in a small town like Eagle Mountain. She kept going over and over the events of the day she had been attacked. Had Carl been in the grocery store that day, too? Had he followed her back to the ranch?

But if Carl was targeting her, why would he do so? The bank robbery had occurred almost nine years ago. Bette had been out of prison eight months. If Eddie had been serious about exacting revenge for her testimony at his trial, surely he would have acted long before now.

Still, it seemed too much of a coincidence that Carl should be in Eagle Mountain, just when so many bad things had happened to her. Had Carl stolen Lacy's and Travis's wedding rings and hidden them in her cabin? She shook her head. That didn't make sense, either. Carl would have kept the rings for himself. From what she remembered, he had a taste for theft. He had even bragged about things he had stolen, the way other men might boast about their times in a marathon or deals they had closed at work. Then again, theft was Carl's work. As far as Bette knew, he had never held a legitimate job—something he had in common with Eddie, though she hadn't realized it at the time.

She was still pondering all this when Travis and Cody returned to the ranch. Everyone else had finished supper, so the two men ate the food Rainey had saved for them and recounted their afternoon's work. "We tracked Carl to the motel in town," Travis said. "But by the time we got there, he had checked out."

"He registered under the name of Charlie Fergusen and paid cash," Cody said. "But the clerk recognized him when we showed her his photograph."

"She says he checked in two days ago," Travis said. "Shortly after the road closed. He said he was passing through and got stranded."

Bette's heart sank. "If he's not at the motel, where is he?" she asked.

"Is the road open again?" Lacy asked.

"Nope." Travis finished the last bite of roast beef. "Which means he found somewhere else to stay. Maybe he heard we were looking for him."

"Or he figured since Bette and Lacy saw him, it was time to hide out," Cody said.

"Every one of my deputies has his description and photograph and will be watching for him," Travis said. "So do all the ranch hands. He won't get near the ranch without us knowing."

"Thank you," Bette said. "I... I don't know what to say. If I brought this trouble to you and your family—"

"You didn't do anything wrong," Travis said. "If this man intends to cause trouble, that's on him." His eyes met hers. "You're my guest and my wife's friend. I'm going to make sure you're protected. I'm sorry if I didn't make that clear before."

Bette read the determination and sincerity in his eyes and in that moment thought she knew what Lacy saw in this serious, quiet lawman. She nodded and turned away, aware as she did so of Cody watching her, just as he had watched her in Travis's office. He was serious and quiet, too, but harder for her to interpret than the sheriff. How could he have made such passionate love to her one night, and stood by saying nothing while Travis accused her of taking those rings? Whatever feelings he had for her, they weren't enough to overcome his suspicions—or his desire to look good in front of his friend. He wasn't that different from Eddie, really—the kind of man who would always put his own best interests ahead of any woman.

Chapter Thirteen

Bette returned to her cabin after breakfast the next morning, and found Cody waiting on the front porch.

He rose from the chair where he had been sitting. "I wanted to talk to you," he said.

She did not want to talk to him. What could she possibly say to him? When he refused to defend her to Travis, she had known what people meant when they talked about a broken heart. It had felt that way, that night in her cabin, a great, tearing pain in her chest.

"You shouldn't be here," she said. "I don't have anything to say—" She stopped, the incongruity of his presence here hitting her. "How did you get in here?" she asked. "I locked the door when I went to breakfast."

He held up a key, identical to the one in her hand. "There are at least three of them for every cabin," he said. "In a box in the drawer of Mr. Walker's desk, where anyone can help himself."

She shut the door behind her and sat on the side of the bed, while he once more took the chair she had almost begun to think of as his. "Why do they have so many keys?" she asked.

"When they built the cabins, they had the idea to rent them out to tourists—sort of a cowboy guest ranch," he said. "They had multiple keys made so that they could give out more than one if, say, a couple stayed in a cabin, and in case someone lost a key."

"How did you find out about the keys?"

"I asked Travis. And I told him about the paint on your door and the paint you found in the bathroom. I know you didn't want me to say anything about that, but I wanted him to know it was possible someone got into your cabin—using a spare key—and planted those rings there."

She eyed him warily. Cody had actually defended her? And Travis had listened? "Did he believe you?"

"He was open to the possibility."

Do you believe me? But she had too much pride to ask the question. "So I know how you got in," she said. "What are you doing here?"

"I came to ask you to go ice fishing with me."

She definitely hadn't seen that one coming. "Ice fishing?"

"Yes. There's a lake on Forest Service land near here that Nate Hall assures me has good fishing. We can use one of the snowmobiles to get there." He actually looked excited about the idea.

"Why would I want to go ice fishing?" she asked. "With you?"

"It's a beautiful day. And I don't want to go fishing by myself."

"Then ask Travis or one of the ranch hands to go with you." She folded her arms across her chest. "Or is this your idea of keeping an eye on me—trailing after me like you trail after one of the fugitives you intend to apprehend?"

He flinched, but she couldn't feel very victorious about the hit. Sitting here with him, in such familiar postures, made her ache for what they had had between them. How perverse was it that she could hate him—and at the same time want to jump his body? She stood. "You need to leave."

He stood also, but instead of moving toward the door, he moved toward her. "Look," he said. "I'm sorry about the other night. You don't want to hear it, but I am."

"You didn't even try to defend me!" She couldn't keep the words back, or the venom behind them. "You stood there while he accused me of a horrible betrayal of my best friend, and you wouldn't even look at me. And you helped him paw through my things, as if I was some common criminal—because that's all that I am to you."

"Bette, no." He took her by the arms. She tried to pull away, but he held on, gentle, yet unyielding. "Look at me," he said.

She looked, and was surprised to see pain in his eyes. "I'm a cop," he said. "It's what I do. What I've trained to do for years. That night, I wasn't here as your lover, I was here as a cop. I had to put aside emotion and consider the evidence as dispassionately as possible."

"So I didn't matter at all—only the evidence."

"That's what I've been taught." He slid his hands down, until they encircled her wrists, his touch burning into her. "But I learned something important that night."

She couldn't help it, he mesmerized her. This must be what the mouse felt before it was swallowed by the viper. "What did you learn?"

"That I'm not the stone-cold, by-the-book cop I always thought I was. You do matter. And it didn't make any difference what my brain told me when I looked at the evidence, my heart shouted something different. That's why I told Travis about the paint, and went looking for the key."

She wanted to believe him, more than she had ever wanted to believe anyone. Her gaze shifted to his lips, and she leaned in closer, wanting to feel their touch, to taste him, to breathe him in and…

She pulled away. "I don't know if I can trust you," she said.

"I understand that. But come fishing with me today anyway."

"Why?"

"Because you're smart. And I'm smart, too. And I think the two of us can figure this out. Whoever put those rings in your cabin wanted to get you into trouble. I figure if we spend some time away from the ranch and all the tension here, just the two of us doing something mindless like fishing, it might come to us how and why they did it—and maybe even who."

He released her wrists and stepped back. "The Walkers are having a new lock put on your cabin today," he said. "With only one key, which they'll give to you. It would be a good idea if you got away for a few hours so they can do the work."

"So I guess I might as well come with you," she said. "But just so you know—fish are the only thing you're going to catch today."

The lines around his eyes tightened, and she wondered if he was trying not to laugh at her. "Understood."

APPARENTLY, ICE FISHING required donning a pair of thick insulated coveralls and round-toed insulated rubber boots that made prison uniforms look like high fashion, and a helmet that weighed as much as a Thanksgiving turkey. "Are we going fishing or visiting the moon?" Bette asked when she was thus dressed.

"You don't want to get cold, do you?" Cody asked.

"Why would anyone want to do anything where you have to dress like this?" she asked, as she climbed onto the back of the snowmobile he had parked in front of her cabin.

"Because it's fun."

"Standing around a hole in the ice waiting for a fish to get hungry enough to eat a worm does not sound like my idea of fun," she said.

"Sure it is." He climbed on the snowmobile in front of her and punched the button to start the engine. It roared to life, shaking every part of her. "Hang on!" he shouted over the rumbling noise, then they shot forward.

She clung to him, her heart in her throat, but after a few hundred yards she began to relax a little and enjoy the sensation of racing over the snow. Cody whooped and steered the machine through the trees, which sped by in a blur of white and green. They roared up an incline, then plunged across an iced-over creek. It was like riding a motorcycle, only better, since they didn't have to follow a road. They could pick any path they liked over the deep snow, though she realized after a while that Cody was following orange markers blazed on the trees.

Half an hour or so later, he slowed the machine. He gestured toward a frozen lake in the distance, the ice a blue mirror reflecting the surrounding evergreens. After a few minutes, the lake disappeared from view. Cody halted the snowmobile in a clearing. Bette's ears rang in the sudden silence. They climbed off the snowmobile and removed their helmets. "You know how they say getting there is half the fun?" she asked.

"Yeah," he said.

"I think in this case, it was all the fun." She grinned. "That was a blast."

"You've never been on a snowmobile before?"

"No."

"Then after we're done fishing I'll take you the long way home."

"I want to drive," she said.

"No." He pocketed the keys. "You just told me you've never even been on one of these things before."

"I'm a quick learner. Besides, how hard could it be? They rent them to tourists."

He opened a compartment on the back of the snowmobile and took out some disassembled fishing poles, a tackle box, two plastic buckets and what looked like an oversize drill. He fitted the sections of the poles together, handed the poles and tackle to her, then shouldered the drill and picked up the buckets. "What is that thing on your shoulder?" she asked.

"Ice auger. We just have to hike through those trees and up that little rise to reach the lakeshore." He strode toward the trees and she tromped through the snow after him. As the woods thinned, the lake came into view once more, heavy snow on its shore giving way to thick ice. Out on the ice, Cody lowered the auger. "As soon as I drill a hole with this, we can fish," he said.

"Excuse me if I don't stand around watching," she said. She returned to shore and began following a trail around the edge. Hoofprints in the snow showed where deer had walked along the edge of the lake, perhaps searching for open water to drink. She couldn't see the snowmobile from here, which made her feel all the more isolated. When she had gone some ways, she turned and looked back toward Cody. He was attacking the ice with the auger, all his concentration on the task.

I'm a cop. It's what I do. What did that mean—to be a cop? If someone had asked her that question a year ago, when she was still in prison, she would have said cops went after people who committed crimes—and a lot of people who didn't. She would have pointed out that cops too often locked someone up because it was easy to make a case against them, and that they were more interested in cadging free doughnuts from the coffee shop than finding out the truth.

There were still some cops like that, she believed. But there was another kind, too. Travis had worked hard to get to the truth and free Lacy, long before she fell in love with him. His brother, Gage, seemed to be a man who tried to do what was right.

Then there was Cody—who had refrained from killing a desperate man, only to have that man commit suicide right in front of him. The pain she had seen in his eyes when he had told her that story, and the pain she recognized when he had apologized to her, had been real, mirroring her own hurt. She believed he was trying to see past the evidence and his training to her innocence. But was that going to be enough?

He set aside the auger, then spotted her and motioned her to come back to him. She retraced her steps around the pond and out onto the ice. He handed her a fishing pole, then turned one of the buckets upside down and set it beside the hole. "Make yourself comfortable and drop your line in," he said.

She sat on the bucket and plopped the end of the weighted line into the water, where it sank out of sight. Cody sat on the other bucket beside her. "Isn't this fun?" she said, heavy on the sarcasm.

"It's a beautiful day," Cody said. "We're out in the fresh air, we might catch some fish for supper and we're alone."

Right. Alone at last. "Then let's talk about who stole those wedding rings and put them in my cabin," she said.

"Almost anyone at the ranch could have taken the key from Mr. Walker's desk and let himself into your cabin," Cody said. "Just as many people had access to Travis's bedroom, where he kept the rings."

"It would be easier on everyone if the thief wasn't someone on the ranch, but an outsider," Bette said. Another reason suspicion had focused on her.

"Someone like Carl Wayland," Cody said.

"Yes, but I don't see how Carl—or Charlie, or whatever name he's going by these days—could have slipped into the house unnoticed, taken the key and the wedding rings and stashed them in my cabin," she said. "There are always too many people around. Besides, why carry out such a complicated plot to implicate me?"

"I agree," Cody said. "I still think Doug or Rainey is the most likely candidate for that, though I can't think why. Even given that they're jealous of you, or want to cater the wedding themselves, that kind of behavior doesn't make sense. They risk too much for too little gain."

"I agree," Bette said.

"Is there someone else who wants you away from the ranch, but is being more subtle about it?" Cody asked. "Do you have an ex-lover among the ranch hands? Or someone you double-crossed in prison who wants to get back at you? Are you the long-lost daughter of the duke who has come to claim her birthright and the family fortune?"

She laughed. "I guess those theories made as much sense as anything I can come up with."

His expression grew more serious. "Let's put aside the ring theft for a while. What about the person who attacked you with the big rock on your way home from town? Still no memory of that?"

"No. I'm wondering if I should try being hypnotized or something. I can't remember anything."

"But it could have been Carl?"

"Yes," she said. "That attack strikes me as more his style."

"Why would he want to hurt you?"

"He was friends with Eddie. Eddie swore he'd kill me if I gave the police any information about the gang or the robbery."

"So you think maybe Eddie sent him here to make good on his threat?" Cody asked.

She shifted the fishing pole in her hand. "I don't know. That doesn't make a lot of sense to me, either. By the time the police arrested me, they already had everyone but the getaway driver, and I didn't know anything about him. Nothing I told the police made things worse for Eddie. I never talked to him again after the day of the robbery, but he could have easily gotten a message to me if he wanted to threaten me again or remind me of his promise. I've been out of prison eight months and nothing has happened to make me feel like I'm in danger."

"Until you showed up here." He sat forward on his bucket. "I think I got a bite."

A few seconds later, he was scooping a large trout into a net and depositing it on the ice between them. "Dinner," he said, and grinned at her.

While he took care of the fish and rebaited his hook, she thought about Carl. "When I saw Carl in the grocery store, he didn't seem surprised to see me," she said. "Maybe that's because he did come to Eagle Mountain to look for me."

"Was a lot of money taken in that robbery?" Cody asked. "Maybe Carl thinks Eddie gave the loot to you and he wants his share."

She shook her head. "The bank got all the money back. The police caught Eddie and the others before they even had a chance to divide it up."

"Why didn't they catch the driver?" Cody asked.

"I guess he wasn't at the apartment the afternoon the police showed up. I really don't know, since I wasn't there, either. They arrested me later, after they learned of my relationship with Eddie. They already knew someone had shut off the alarm system and left the back door unlocked." She hung her head. "You don't know how many times I've regretted doing those things. I knew they were wrong, but Eddie had persuaded me the ends justified the means. I was so stupid."

"You paid for your mistake," he said.

"I did." She gripped the fishing pole tighter. "I've worked really hard to build a new life for myself, and I wouldn't risk throwing all that away by stealing a couple of wedding rings— especially rings that belong to a woman who's done everything she could to help me."

"I believe you," Cody said.

She stared at him. "You're willing to overlook the evidence and take my word for it?"

"I'm not overlooking the evidence," he said. "The rings were hidden in an obvious location. You're not that dumb. If you had taken them, you would have locked them in your suitcase or tucked them under the eaves or, I don't know, sewn them into your bra. You wouldn't have put them where we could find them so easily."

"Maybe I believed you wouldn't look," she said.

"You let us search your cabin without a warrant. Even an innocent person might not have done that. Again—you're not stupid."

"Thank you. I think."

"I convinced the Walkers not to tell anyone about the new lock on your cabin," he said. "They're going to leave the spare keys in the desk, just like before, and Travis is setting up a hidden video camera in the office, focused on the desk. If anyone comes to take the key again, we'll catch them."

"Then I hope they do come," Bette said. She cleared her throat. "And thank you. You're going to a lot of trouble to clear my name. Travis, too, I guess."

"We want to catch the right person," he said. "The worst thing that can happen, as a law enforcement officer, is to find out you helped put an innocent person behind bars. It makes you doubt everything about yourself and the job."

"I guess I never thought about that," she said. "I only saw things from the point of view of the innocent person—someone like Lacy."

"Sometimes cops are victims of their own zeal to close a case," he said. "Or we get fooled by the evidence. It can happen easier than you think."

"Has it ever happened to you?"

"No. And knowing it can happen makes me more careful." His eyes met hers. "I don't want you to be my first mistake."

She looked away, warmed by his words, but too unsure to speak. She wanted to believe Cody had her best interests at heart, but she had learned the hard way that her hormones could overrule good sense. She didn't want to make the same mistake again.

She cleared her throat and turned to him. "Why a cop?" she asked. "I mean, why would you want a job that puts you in contact with so many dangerous, unpleasant people?"

"Why did you want to be a caterer?"

"Because I like to cook, I like parties and it's something I'm really good at."

"It's sort of the same thing with me." He pulled up his line and checked the hook, then lowered it into the water again. "I started out wanting to be a lawyer. I liked the idea of putting away criminals, and television shows and books make it seem really glamorous. By the time I graduated and started prepping to take the bar exam, I'd figured out it was a lot duller than most people know. Then I met a guy who worked for the US Marshals Service and he told me they were hiring, and that with my law degree, I'd have one up on a lot of candidates. I decided to apply, maybe do the job for a couple of years before I took the bar exam." He shrugged. "I got hooked and never looked back."

"Do you ever think about doing anything else—maybe taking the bar?" she asked.

He hesitated before answering. "I never used to," he said. "Now… I don't know. Maybe someday. I guess seeing somebody blow his brains out right in front of you gives you a different perspective on the job."

She put her hand on his arm and kept it there. "I guess law enforcement needs people like you," she said. "But you'd probably make a good lawyer, too."

"The path we choose when we're young doesn't have to be the one we stay on our whole lives." His eyes met hers, and she had the sense of seeing the real man, with no defensive screens. "People can change."

He was telling her he believed she had changed, and her heart felt too big for her chest as the idea sank in. This hard-nosed cop was telling her that—maybe—he was learning to see past the mistakes she had made.

Maybe even into a future where a woman like her and a man like him might be together.

BY THE TIME the sun began sinking behind the trees, Cody and Bette had caught five good-sized fish. He cleaned them and packed them in snow in one of the buckets, then they gathered their gear and headed back toward the snowmobile.

They were still a few dozen yards from the machine when Cody halted, frowning. Bette set down the tackle box and followed his gaze toward the snowmobile. "What is it?" she asked.

He shook his head and started forward again. Twenty yards farther on, Cody stopped again and set down the auger and the bucket of fish. He motioned for Bette to stay back and he approached the snowmobile.

The snow around the machine had been churned up. The snowmobile's hood lay in the snow a few feet beyond them, and Bette could see wires sticking up out of the engine compartment. Cody carefully circled the machine, then scanned the area around them. "What's wrong?" Bette called when she could bear the tension of his silence no more.

"Someone's wrecked it," he said. "On purpose." He gestured toward the dangling wires. "They've cut the wiring harness."

"What are we going to do?" she asked.

He pulled out his phone and took photographs of the damage, and of the ground around the snowmobile. "No service," he said, checking the screen. "We'll have to walk back."

She looked past the snowmobile, at the faint track they had made getting to this place. "How far is it?" she asked.

"About five miles." He moved the bucket of fish and the auger closer to the snowmobile, and took the poles and tackle from her to add to the pile. "Come on," he said. "We'd better get started if we want to make it back before dark."

Chapter Fourteen

The trek back to the ranch was brutal, postholing through snow up past the knees. They hadn't traveled half a mile before Cody was sweating inside the thick insulated coverall, and the rubber boots that were fine for snowmobiling and fishing felt as if they weighed ten pounds each. Bette was having a hard time, too, though she didn't utter a word of complaint. He tried to break trail for her, but that didn't make the going much easier.

He had remembered to grab a water bottle from the snowmobile, and he stopped after what he judged to be the first mile and handed it to her. She drank deeply and returned it to him. "How do you know we're headed in the right direction?" she asked.

"I'm following our path here, and the blazes on the trees." He indicated the orange plastic diamonds affixed to tree trunks at regular intervals.

She nodded. "So, is this just another prank to annoy me—like the message on my door?"

"The lake is on National Forest land," Cody said. "It's possible someone came along and decided to mess with the snowmobile—malicious mischief."

"Why didn't we see them—or hear them?"

"I think they parked in the woods and walked in," Cody said. "We were out of sight over the hill, and the sound wouldn't necessarily have carried that far. They wouldn't have had to make a lot of noise."

"Maybe I'm being paranoid, but I think this was directed at me," she said. "It kind of fits with a pattern of harassment."

"Would Carl do something like this?"

"I have no idea. Maybe. I didn't know the man. I didn't want to know him."

"When Travis finds him, he can follow up on his alibi for this afternoon."

"If he finds him," she said.

He stashed the water bottle in one of the pockets of his coat. "Come on. Let's keep walking." But before he could take even another step forward, something whistled past his ear, followed by the distinctive popping sound of weapons fire.

"Get down!" He shoved Bette into the snow and threw himself on top of her, as bullets continued to strike around them. "Into the trees," he said and shoved her forward. Scrambling in the deep snow, they headed for a stand of fir, fifty yards to their left, away from the direction of the shots. They moved clumsily through the thick snow, clawing their way toward cover as bullets continued to rain down. Cody tried to keep himself between Bette and the shooter, staying low to present a smaller target and moving erratically when possible. They had almost reached cover when the impact of a bullet propelled him forward. Burning pain radiated from his shoulder as he fell, but he kept moving, crawling after Bette, into the trees. They lay at the base of one of the evergreens, gasping.

Grimacing, Cody raised up enough to unzip his coverall and draw his Glock, though the movement cost him. His right shoulder felt as if someone had rammed a hot poker through it, and he could feel blood dripping down his back.

"You're hurt!" Bette stared at his shoulder, her face almost as white as the surrounding snow.

He sat back against the tree, keeping his weight on his good side, and closed his eyes a moment, gearing up for what he knew he'd have to do next.

Bette crawled up beside him. "Let me see," she said.

He angled his body so that she could look. "I think the bullet is still in there," he said. "How much blood is there?"

"Not as much as I would have thought," she said. "It's more seeping than gushing. That's good, I think."

He nodded. It was good—as long as the bullet hadn't nicked some internal artery. But he didn't think so. "How are you at first aid?" he asked.

"I can put a Band-Aid on a boo-boo," she said. "I think this requires more than that."

"If I was the kind of man who carried a clean white handkerchief everywhere, we could use it as a bandage," he said.

She studied the wound again. "I guess what we're looking for is something clean that can soak up the blood and protect the wound from dirt, right?"

"Right."

"Then I have something." She turned her back to him and unzipped her coveralls. A few deft movements later, she pulled out her bra and dangled it in front of his face. "It's padded and it's mostly cotton. And it's clean."

He choked back a laugh. "You're amazing, you know that?"

"I'm practical. It's not the same thing. Now turn around."

He grit his teeth and cried out only once as she doused the wound with the rest of the water from their bottle, then twisted and wrapped the bra into an awkward bandage. "It looks ridiculous, but I think it will serve our purposes," she said. "Now what?"

"Now we try to find a way out of here," he said. The gunfire had stopped, leaving the area silent—the unnatural silence after violence has intruded.

Bette followed his gaze to the open area they had just crossed. "He was waiting for us," she said in a ragged whisper. "Watching us. He let us get away from the snowmobile, out in the open, and when we stopped, he tried to kill us."

"It looks that way." Cody checked his gun to make sure it was loaded—it was always loaded, but this gave him something to do with his hands, since whoever had put them in this situation wasn't close enough to strangle.

Bette closed her eyes, then opened them again. "This is crazy. I just need to find Carl and ask him what he wants. That's what I should have done in the grocery store that day, instead of running away."

"Maybe this isn't Carl," Cody said.

She stared at him. "You don't think it's Doug? Or Rainey?"

"Maybe it's the Ice Cold Killer."

"He's a serial killer. He ambushes women and cuts their throats."

"He didn't cut your throat," Cody said. "You're unfinished business." The more he thought about it, the more it made sense to him. Yes, the attack on Bette hadn't been the killer's usual style, but that might be a sign that he was getting desperate. Coming unhinged. Considering that it took a kind of mental imbalance to become a serial killer in the first place, was it so far-fetched to think that could progress into an obsession with one particular woman? "Maybe he's been waiting for another chance and thought this was it."

"So what do we do now?" she asked. "Lie here and wait for him to come after us?"

"I think we wait and see what he does next."

"I am not going to lie here and let him pick us off like shooting fish in a barrel," she said. She started to rise but wasn't to her feet yet when a bullet hit the tree trunk above her head, sending bark flying.

With a yelp, she flattened herself on the ground once more. "Okay, I guess that was stupid," she muttered.

Cody studied the landscape beyond this

stand of trees. A small rise, slightly above and to the left, would provide good cover for the shooter. "I think he's in the rocks up there," he said, indicating the spot. "I don't think he can see us here, but he probably knows he hit me. He's waiting to see what we do next."

"Can you shoot him from here?" she asked.

"No. He's using a rifle. My handgun isn't going to do us any good unless he gets closer." He nudged her. "Let's start moving back, deeper into the woods. He won't be able to get a clear shot at us, and he may have to expose himself to come after us."

They crawled backward twenty, then thirty feet, to the banks of a frozen creek that wound through the trees. Cody moved awkwardly, trying and failing to protect his wounded shoulder, so that by the time they reached the creek, he was dizzy from pain. When he could speak, he said, "If we move along this creek, we'll be headed toward the ranch, but we'll still have cover."

"It's going to take all night to get back to the ranch, crawling on our hands and knees," she said. "And you need a doctor."

Cody didn't tell her they probably didn't have all night. A killer who had followed them to the lake, sabotaged their snowmobile, then waited patiently for them to provide clear targets wasn't going to stop his pursuit now. All Cody could do was try to make the task more difficult for him. Keeping in the shelter of the trunk of a large fir, he rose to his knees, then stood. All remained silent. "Come on. It will be easier walking."

They moved alongside the creek, climbing over snowbanks and skirting deadfall. No one fired on them, but Cody had the sensation that they were still being watched. Was the shooter waiting for them to emerge into the open again?

And then they were almost out of cover, the woods giving way to a broad meadow, snow like icing over a sheet cake. He stopped ten yards from the last tree. "We can't cross that," Bette whispered.

Cody scanned the surroundings, looking for the shooter's vantage point. He saw half a dozen possibilities. He needed to draw the man out, make him show his hand. He had no chance if he didn't know where the shots would come from. But Bette was right—stepping into that open field would be suicide.

"When we don't come back for supper, someone from the ranch will come looking for us," Bette said. "They knew we were coming here to fish."

It was anyone's guess how long that would take. By himself, Cody might have hazarded more direct action, but he couldn't risk Bette. "Then I guess we wait," he said.

He made himself as comfortable as possible—which wasn't very comfortable, his back to a tree, the gun in his right hand, trying to ignore the throbbing pain in his left shoulder and arm. Bette sat beside him, one hand on his thigh. She kept glancing at his injured shoulder. "What?" he asked, the tenth time she looked.

"The blood is seeping through," she said.

"I hope it wasn't your favorite bra," he said.

"If you'd ever had to wear one, you'd know there is no such thing," she said.

"I think I can speak for most men when I say you never have to wear one on our account."

A twig snapped, and they both sat up straighter. His hand tightened on the Glock.

"Maybe it's just a deer," she whispered.

A bullet thudded into a tree five feet in front of them. "Last time I checked, deer didn't carry rifles," Cody said, as he urged her to the ground. He peered around the trunk of the tree. Was that movement there, behind those rocks? He fired, and shards of rock flew from a boulder at the front of the grouping, followed by a volley of gunfire in their direction.

He flattened himself on the ground over Bette. "You're crushing me," she said, her face in the dirt.

"Better flattened than dead."

"And people say chivalry is dead."

"If I could get a little closer, I'd have a better chance of hitting him," he said.

She clutched his arm. "No. He'll kill you."

"Not if I'm careful."

"No," she said again. "Don't leave me."

"I won't." He realized he couldn't. If the gunman did kill him, she'd be left helpless. The shooter fired sporadically for the next ten minutes, with Cody returning fire. Then the hammer clicked onto an empty cylinder. He sagged to the ground behind the tree again and tried to move his left hand toward the spare ammo clip on his belt. It was impossible.

"What are you doing?" Bette asked.

"I need you to get the ammo clip off my belt," he said.

She fumbled a little, but managed to unfasten the clip. "Aren't you Mr. Prepared?" she said.

"Aren't you glad I am?"

"Oh, I am." She levered herself up and kissed him, hard. "I'm very glad."

The roar of an engine—more than one engine, Cody decided—broke the stillness that had followed the last volley of gunfire. Headlights swept the edge of the forest. Breaking twigs and muffled steps announced the shooter's retreat. Cody waited, heart pounding painfully. Beside him, Bette breathed raggedly.

"Cody! It's Travis! Are you okay?"

"In here!" Bette stood and waved, then moved toward their voices. Cody closed his eyes and sagged against the tree. They were safe. For now, anyway.

Chapter Fifteen

"Travis, I've never been so glad to see anyone in my life." Bette grabbed the sheriff by the arm and dragged him toward the tree where she and Cody had been sheltering. "Cody's hurt. He needs a doctor right away."

"What happened?" Mr. Walker strode up behind his son.

"Someone sabotaged our snowmobile, so we had to walk out," Bette said. "Then they started shooting at us. They hit Cody." They had reached the tree.

Travis knelt beside Cody. "Hey."

Cody scowled at him. "Hey yourself. About time you got here."

"Bette said somebody shot you."

"Rifle shot. It didn't bleed too much."

"Let me take a look." He helped Cody sit forward, and he shined the light on the blood-stained bandage. He frowned. "What is that you've got on there?" he asked.

"A padded bra," Bette said, her tone daring him to say something about it.

"Any idea who was doing the shooting?" Travis asked.

"Never got a look at him," Cody said. "He fired on us first in the open, then followed us in here. He had us pinned down while he was shooting from behind those rocks." He gestured toward the shooter's location. "I kept him from getting any closer, then you scared him off."

"I need you to wait here while I take a look," Travis said.

"I'm not going anywhere."

Mr. Walker stayed with them while Travis went to investigate the rock outcropping. "When you didn't show up for supper, we figured your snowmobile might have broken down," Mr. Walker said.

"Someone cut the wiring harness," Cody said. "It shouldn't be too hard to fix."

"I'm not too worried about that machine right now, son," Mr. Walker said. He turned to Bette. "How about you? Are you okay?"

"I am now," she said. "You arrived just in time."

The approaching beam of Travis's flashlight signaled his return. "I didn't find much," he said. "Some impressions in the snow. We'll come back in the morning and take a better look. It's getting too dark to track anybody right now."

"Whoever it was is probably long gone," Cody said.

Travis handed his father the flashlight and moved to Cody's other side. "Can you walk?" he asked.

"I can walk," Cody said. With Travis's help, he staggered up. Bette followed, Mr. Walker bringing up the rear. Travis helped Cody onto his snowmobile, then Bette climbed on behind his dad.

The return trip to the ranch had none of the joy of the morning's journey. Bette held on to Mr. Walker, teeth chattering as icy wind buffeted her, her gaze fixed on the dark shadow of Cody's back on the snowmobile just ahead.

As they neared the ranch, Travis slowed. "We've got a phone signal now," Mr. Walker called over his shoulder. "He's phoning ahead for help."

Fifteen minutes later, they arrived at the ranch house, where a small crowd waited to greet them. "An ambulance is on the way," Travis said. "Let's get inside, where it's warm."

Bette climbed off the snowmobile, stiff with cold. She tried to move toward Cody, but Lacy put her arm around her and steered her toward the house. "You're half-frozen," she said. "Come in here by the fire."

"Cody—" Bette looked over her shoulder.

"I've got Cody," Travis said. "Go inside."

Too worn out to argue, Bette let Lacy lead her into the house and help her out of the bulky helmet, coveralls and boots. She sighed with relief as Lacy tucked her under a blanket in a chair by the fire. A few second later, Cody came in, leaning on Travis's arm. But he balked at sitting on the sofa. "I'm not going to bleed on your furniture," he said.

Mr. Walker brought a chair from the dining table and Cody lowered himself gingerly into it. His face was gray, tight with pain. Bette hurt, looking at him, but she couldn't tear her eyes away. She couldn't forget the way he had lain on top of her, protecting her body with his own. "Where is the ambulance?" she asked.

"It's coming," Lacy said.

"What happened?" Emily asked. "Travis didn't give a lot of details when he called."

"Someone wrecked the snowmobile, then started shooting at us," Cody said. "He had us pinned down behind a tree when the cavalry arrived and scared him off."

"Who would do something like that?" Emily asked.

"If I knew the answer to that, I sure wouldn't be sitting here right now," Cody said.

The strident wail of the ambulance stopped

all conversation. Mr. Walker went outside to direct them and moments later two paramedics came in and began examining Cody.

Lacy handed Bette a mug and pulled a chair closer to her. "Are you okay?" she asked. "No wounds or frostbite or anything that needs seeing to?"

"No, I'm fine." She sipped the mug, which turned out to be hot chocolate, heavily laced with peppermint schnapps. Soothing warmth spread through her.

"That must have been terrifying," Lacy said.

"Yes." The fear still hadn't left her. They both might have been killed. No. She couldn't think about that. They were safe. They were going to be okay.

Cody let out a sharp cry and she had to set the mug on the table beside her, her hands shook so violently. Then the paramedics helped him onto a waiting stretcher and draped blankets over him.

Travis came and bent over Bette. "They're taking him to the clinic in town to have the bullet removed," he said. "I'm going to go with him. Is there anything else you can tell me about the guy who shot at you?"

She shook her head. "We never saw him. Cody said he had a rifle. He followed us for a while. I think he was waiting for us to come out into the open again, then he came in after us. I don't know who he is, I swear."

"Doug and Rainey both served supper tonight," Travis said. "So it wasn't them. We're still trying to find Carl Wayland."

"Call us after Cody comes out of surgery," Lacy said.

"I will." He kissed her goodbye and left.

"Drink your chocolate," Lacy said. "I'll bring you something to eat."

"I don't think I could eat," Bette said.

"Then I'll bring it and you can pick at it."

After she left, Bette leaned back in the chair and closed her eyes. She had thought the events of the afternoon would replay in her head but instead the image that came to her was of Cody, bringing up that first fish and giving her a look of triumph—the kind of look friends would share.

The kind of look she thought she would like to see over and over again. For the rest of her life.

CODY CALLED THE sheriff's department the next morning just after eight. Adelaide answered and when Cody said he wanted to speak to the sheriff, she informed him that Travis was still at the ranch, probably eating breakfast. "He was out on a call very late last night," she said.

"I know," said Cody. "I was that call."

"Marshal Rankin, is that you?" Adelaide asked. "How are you doing?"

"I'm sore and grumpy and don't intend to stay in this clinic one minute longer than necessary."

"I don't know what you expect the sheriff to do about that."

"I want him to come get me and take me back to the ranch. But since he's not there—Adelaide, everyone knows you really run that department. Can't you send a deputy over to get me?"

"This is a sheriff's department, not a taxi service."

"I'm an officer of the law, so consider it an interagency favor." No response. He resorted to begging. "Please, Adelaide. They don't even make decent coffee in this place and I had to threaten the nurse to get her to bring me my clothes."

"I'll see what I can do."

Ten minutes later, Gage walked into the clinic. He grinned when he saw Cody, who was sitting on the edge of the narrow clinic bed, his shoulder swathed in bandages. "I figured your shirt was trashed, so I brought you this." He held out a Rayford County Sheriff sweatshirt. "Size extra-large, so it should fit over those bandages."

"Thanks." Cody stood and began struggling into the shirt. Gage moved over to help him. "Let's get out of here," Cody said, when he was dressed.

When they were in the cruiser, Gage handed him a large cup of coffee. "Adelaide sent this," he said.

"Bless her." He popped the lid and drank deeply.

"She said you were a real bear on the phone. Want to tell me why?"

"Oh, I don't know. Having a divot taken out of my shoulder and trying to sleep in that clinic on that narrow bed, and nobody telling me anything about what is going on—I think that would put anyone in a bad mood."

"Normally we send gunshot victims to the hospital in Junction," Gage said. "The clinic isn't really set up for surgery. And from what I hear, you were lucky. The bullet just missed shattering your shoulder blade."

Cody grunted and drank more coffee. He began to feel more human. "How is Bette?" he asked.

Gage glanced at him. "Was she shot, too?"

"No. I just… I just wondered how she's doing."

"I haven't heard. You can ask her yourself

when you get to the ranch. I called and let Travis know you were coming."

"Any sign of Carl Wayland?"

"Nope. But unless he hiked out, he's still here. Last avalanche on the pass took out a bunch of power lines—poles and line strung all over the highway, under about ten feet of packed snow and rock. It's going to take a while to fix that mess."

Another grunt from Cody. That seemed to be the best he could do at the moment. His shoulder hurt like the devil, but he had refused the pain meds the doctor had prescribed, not wanting to fog his brain. He had lain awake in the early morning hours, replaying everything that happened yesterday. But no matter how many times he went over the puzzle, he couldn't find the missing pieces. That, more than anything, had put him in a bad mood.

At the ranch, Travis came out to meet him, followed by Bette and Lacy. Cody refused Travis's offer of assistance and got out of the car under his own power. He caught Bette's eye and nodded. He was all right. And he was going to make things all right for her.

"Should you be out of the hospital?" Lacy asked.

"There is no hospital," he said. He moved past her. "I can mend here as well as anywhere."

"You look like you're in pain," Bette said, coming alongside him.

"So do you," he said. "What's your excuse?" He winked, to let her know there was no heat behind the words, no matter how gruff they may have sounded. That earned him a smile.

"I'd better get back to work," Gage said. "And I've got a bachelor party to see to."

"I don't think now is a good time for that," Travis said. "We should put it off."

"Moe is closing down the whole pub for us," Gage said. "It won't kill you to take a few hours to say goodbye to single life with your friends."

"Neither you nor Dwight had a bachelor party," Travis said.

"Right. So we're really looking forward to yours. It's too late for you to back out now."

"Besides, you have to get out of the house so we women can have our party," Lacy said.

Gage glanced at Cody. "If you feel up to it, you're still welcome to come," he said. "Since you probably can't drink, you can be our designated driver."

"I'll let you know," Cody said.

When Gage had gone, Travis joined Cody by the fire. "Dad and I went out to the lake again at first light," he said. "We were able to follow tracks we think were the shooter's to that rock outcropping, back to where it looks like he parked a snowmobile. But then we lost him."

"What about your wrecked snowmobile?"

"Dad doesn't think it'll be too hard to fix. We brought home the fish you caught—frozen solid in that bucket."

"Guess we'll take a rain check on that fish fry," Cody said. He pulled a plastic bag from his pocket. "I brought you something."

Travis studied the smashed piece of metal. "The bullet they took out of you?"

"They got a few bone fragments, too, but I didn't think they qualified as evidence." He nodded to the bag. "It's pretty distorted, but you can tell it's a .225 round."

"Maybe it will help, if we ever find anybody to pin this on." He pocketed the bag. "What does the doctor say about your shoulder?"

"I didn't smash my shoulder blade. I didn't slice an artery and bleed out—which I already kind of figured. Didn't tear any major ligaments. Chipped some bone, damaged some muscle. I need physical therapy and for the rest of my life I'll know when a snowstorm is on its way." He blew out a breath. "Two months off work, at least. Maybe three."

"That bites."

"Yeah, well. Maybe I'll take up a hobby."

"I have to go," Travis said. "I'm determined to track down Carl Wayland today."

"I hope you do."

Travis started to walk away, then turned back. "About this party tonight. You really don't have to come."

"Are you kidding? I wouldn't miss it for the world."

BETTE SPENT THE rest of Saturday morning in the kitchen, preparing the food for the tea that evening, glad to have something to keep her busy. She was pulling a sheet of petit fours out of the oven when Rainey came in. Bette braced herself for some criticism or complaint. "What are you making?" Rainey asked.

The question surprised Bette. Rainey sounded genuinely interested. "These are petit fours for Lacy's bridesmaids' tea," she said. "They don't look like much right now, but they will after I decorate them."

"I guess those girls really go for that fancy food," Rainey said. "I never learned how to do all that. All I know is plain cooking."

"Every meal I've had here has been excellent," Bette said, truthfully. "I imagine you make exactly the kinds of meals the family loves."

"Oh, yeah. Cowboys like plain food that'll

stay with them when they're working all day," Rainey said. "Still, it might be nice to know how to do fancy stuff."

"You could learn," Bette said. "You already know how to cook, so it wouldn't take you any time at all to pick up a few new techniques. I could even show you if you like."

"Maybe. Though I don't know if I'd have time. They keep me pretty busy around here."

"I imagine you were glad to have your son come and help you," Bette said.

"I was. Except…"

"Except what?"

"He hasn't been all that much help since you came." She gave Bette a sideways look. "I was hoping you could tell me why."

"What do you mean?" Bette asked.

"It took me a while to figure it out, but it finally come to me—Doug is afraid of you. That's why he avoids you so much."

"Afraid of me?" She stripped off her oven mitts and faced Rainey. "Why would he be afraid of me?"

"I was hoping you could tell me."

Ah. Maybe this explained Rainey's uncharacteristic friendliness. "What makes you think Doug is afraid of me?"

"Just the way he acts. I know my boy. What I can't figure out is why."

"I don't know what to tell you," Bette said. "I haven't done anything to him, I promise. I mean, what could I do?"

"Well, he's always had some strange ideas," Rainey said. "But he's a good boy. He's made some bad choices, but he's promised me he's going to do better."

"Then I hope he will," Bette said. The timer dinged and she pulled the last tray of petit fours out of the oven. "These need to cool before I decorate them. The oven is all yours if you need it to prepare lunch."

"Oh, I made a stew and sandwiches," Rainey said. "We'll be fine."

"I think I'll go see if Lacy needs any help with the decorations for tonight," Bette said. She still wasn't that comfortable with the older woman.

She was crossing the living room when Cody hailed her. "Bette!"

She turned to find him moving toward her. He still wore the sweatshirt over one arm, leaving the other arm free. "Can you help me with something in my cabin?" he asked. "It's supposed to be a surprise for Travis, so I can't really tell Lacy or his folks."

"I'd like to," she said. "But I was going to see if Lacy needed any help with the decorations for her party."

"Emily is helping her," he said. "It sounded to me like they have everything under control."

"All right." She was curious to know this big secret of his.

They collected their coats and crossed to Cody's cabin, which was the twin of Bette's. The only real difference was a large stuffed cow that occupied the chair beside the small table. It was easily three feet long and two feet tall. "Where did you get this?" she asked, hefting the brown-and-white plush beast.

"Gage got it somewhere," Cody said. He slipped out of his coat, then helped her with hers. "This was all his idea—it's a gag gift, for the party tonight."

"You aren't going to the bachelor party, are you?" she said.

"Why not? I can suffer there as well as I can here, and at least there I'll have distractions."

She scowled at him.

"You're cute when you're disgusted with me," he said.

She launched the cow at him. He caught it by one hind leg, grinning. She couldn't help but grin back. "What am I supposed to help you with?" she asked.

He set the cow on the table and picked up a set of deer antlers. "We have to tie these to the cow's head."

"Why?"

"According to Gage, when Travis was twelve, his father and his uncle took him on his first deer hunt. Travis was so nervous and excited he ended up shooting a neighbor's cow. He spent all summer working to pay for that beef."

"Travis did that?" She had a hard time imagining the straight-arrow sheriff ever coloring outside the lines, even as a kid.

"Gage swears it's true."

"And, of course, his brother never let him forget it," she said.

"Of course." Cody picked up a spool of brown ribbon. "I bought this. I figured we could use it to tie on the antlers—but that's kind of hard to do one-handed. And you probably tie a better bow than I do, anyway."

"I ought to tie a bow around your neck," she said, as she took the spool from him.

"Why? Because I led you into an ambush?"

"No! Do you really think I blame you?"

All the teasing and laughter had left his eyes. "I'm trained to track people. I ought to know when someone is tracking me."

"You had no reason to believe anyone would follow us," she said. "Much less attack us. It was a fishing trip. And I was having a good time until the shooting started."

"Me, too." He reached out with his uninjured

arm and pulled her closer, then kissed her. She sank into that kiss, the tension of the past few days easing. She had missed this—she had missed him.

He raised his head and looked into her eyes. "Do you know what one of my favorite memories of yesterday is?"

"What?"

"When you sacrificed your bra to bandage my wounds."

She laughed. "You would say that."

He shaped his hand to her breast, a mock look of disappointment pulling down the corners of his mouth. "You're wearing a bra now."

"I have more than one."

"I'll buy you a new one." He slid his hand around to her back and deftly undid the clasp. "Something low-cut. With lace."

"I might have guessed." The last word came out in a rush of breath as he pulled down the neck of her sweater to expose the tops of her breasts. He began kissing his way along them. "Cody, what are you doing?" she gasped.

"This." He pulled the sweater lower, and dragged his tongue across her nipple. "And this." He addressed the other breast.

"But, um, you're wounded," she said.

"Not where it counts." He unzipped her jeans.

"I'm worried I'm going to hurt you," she said.

"Sex is a great pain reliever," he said. "I think you told me that once."

He was definitely making it hard for her to think straight. Then again, what did she need to think about? She wanted him, and she was more than relieved to be with him again. Making love seemed right. Healing. She slid both hands under the sweatshirt he wore, skimming the taut muscles of his stomach and over his chest. "Let me help you undress."

"Best idea you've had in five minutes."

She helped him out of his clothing, with a minimum amount of pain on his part, and multiple apologies on her part. "Maybe we shouldn't do this," she said, after she managed to get the sweatshirt off over his head.

"We definitely should," he said, and slipped his hand inside her panties to persuade her.

"All right, we should," she agreed, a little breathless. She moved toward the bed, then stopped. "Should you lie down, or should I?" What would hurt less for him?

"I have an idea." He grasped her hips and backed her toward the bed, which, like the one in Bette's room, was an old-fashioned iron-framed model that sat high off the floor. With her sitting on the edge of the bed and him standing, they lined up perfectly.

"Oh." She wrapped her legs around his hips. "Good idea."

He leaned over and reached for the condom packet on the bedside table. "I see now you didn't really want help with that cow," she said. "You planned to seduce me." She took the packet from him and tore it open.

"I still need help with the cow." He kissed the side of her neck. "Later."

She took the condom from the packet and reached for him. "Allow me."

"There are…definitely…some advantages… to being one-handed," he breathed as she rolled on the condom. Then he wrapped his arm around her and drew her to him, kissing her fiercely.

The man knew how to kiss—deftly setting every nerve on fire with the pressure of his lips or the sweep of his tongue. She reveled in the feel of him in her arms, tracing the line of his spine with her fingers, cupping his firm ass. She let out a sigh when he slid into her, and opened her eyes to stare into his as he began to move. She grasped his hips and met him stroke for stroke, watching as passion etched deeper lines on his face and darkened his eyes. Then he raised her legs, tilting her back slightly, and her breathing grew ragged and her vision blurred. She was dimly aware of the bed knocking against the wall, and her own rising cries as a powerful climax shook her. Cody gripped her more tightly and drove harder, until he came with a shout.

They fell back together on the bed. Bette rolled over and he slid up beside her. "Careful of your shoulder," she cautioned.

"What shoulder?" he breathed.

They lay, not speaking, for a long time. She trailed her fingers through his hair, eyes half-closed. "Did you ever think you'd be involved with a former bank robber?" she asked.

"No." He lifted his head to look at her. "Did you ever think you'd take a US marshal as your lover?"

"Never."

"What's going to happen to us?" he asked.

"Someone is trying to hurt me—maybe kill me," she said. "This isn't a great time to talk about the future."

"Call me an optimist," he said. "I think it is."

"Since when is any lawman an optimist?"

"Since I met you." He kissed her cheek. "You have me believing all kinds of improbable things."

Improbable. That's exactly what they were. Yet here they lay, together, and in spite of the fact that her life might be in danger and she didn't know what she should do next, she was happier than she had ever been.

Chapter Sixteen

"I can't believe how beautiful everything turned out." Emily stepped back and admired the array of white-clothed tables, each with a centerpiece of white lilies and silver plumes. The buffet table featured similar arrangements, as well as carved-crystal snowflakes and drifts of glittery fake snow.

"Most of the decorations were Lacy's idea," Bette said. "I stuck to what I know best—food."

"And what food." Emily lifted the plastic wrap off a tray of silver-and-white-frosted petit fours. "They look so good—you don't mind if I take just one, do you?"

"Go ahead," Bette said. "But just one."

Grinning, Emily chose a petit fours and bit it in half. The delight on her face transformed into a grimace. She spit out the cake, choking.

"What is it?" Bette asked. "What's wrong?"

"The cake!" Emily stared at the mangled pastry in her napkin. "I don't mean to criticize but—did you taste these?"

"No. I mean, I did taste the batter, and I sampled the frosting—they were fine."

"This one wasn't fine."

Bette pulled another cake from the tray and bit into it. The bitterness brought tears to her eyes. She spit it out and looked around for water, but there was none. "Someone has done something to my petit fours!" she wailed. She scanned the buffet table. The finger sandwiches and cream puffs were still in the refrigerator. She wouldn't put them out until after the guests arrived. But the scones, chocolate-dipped apricots and hazelnut shortbread were already arranged on the table, covered with plastic wrap. "We'd better taste everything," she said. "The refrigerated food, too."

Looking doubtful, Emily followed Bette down the table. They sampled cakes and scones and cookies, and by the time they reached the end of the table, Emily was smiling again. "Everything else is delicious," she said.

Bette remembered Rainey's interest in the petit fours, and how she had left the cook alone in the kitchen with the cakes while she went to Cody's cabin. She turned and raced toward the kitchen, Emily in pursuit. "Where are you going?" Emily called.

Bette burst into the kitchen. Rainey looked up from the dishes she was washing. "Is something wrong?" she asked.

"You know what's wrong." Bette crowded the other woman against the sink. "What did you put in my petit fours?"

Rainey's eyes widened in fear. "What are you talking about? I didn't touch your petit fours."

"I left you alone with them and you put something in them," Bette said. "You wanted to embarrass me in front of Lacy and her guests, so you ruined them."

Rainey leaned away from her. "I swear I didn't."

"Taste this!" Bette shoved a cake at the older woman.

Hesitantly, Rainey took the cake and put it in her mouth. She immediately made a face and spit it out. "That's horrible! It tastes like pine cleaner."

"Bette." Emily tugged on Bette's arm. "I think Rainey is telling the truth. Why would she doctor your cakes that way?"

"If she didn't do it, her son did." Bette glared at the cook. "Has Doug been in here this afternoon?"

Rainey hesitated. "He helped me with lunch," she said after a pause.

"Did you see him messing with the cakes?" Bette asked.

"No. I swear I didn't." She swallowed. "He asked me about them, and I told them they were petit fours for the party tonight, and that you were coming back later to frost them."

"Was he ever alone in the kitchen after that?" Bette asked.

Rainey looked panicked. "Maybe," she said. "But why would he ruin your beautiful cakes? And try to ruin Lacy's party? He likes Lacy."

"But he doesn't like me," Bette said. "And you said he's afraid of me. He would like me to leave here."

Rainey hung her head. "He was in here alone while I cleared the table. When I came back, he was acting funny. He left before we had even finished the washing. He told me he had something he needed to do."

"Where is he now?" Emily asked.

"In his room, I guess," Rainey said.

"We'd better talk to him," Bette said.

Rainey led the way up a set of back stairs, to a room at the rear of the house. She knocked on the door, but there was no answer. "Doug?" she called. "Doug, it's Mom. Please open the door."

Silence. Rainey frowned. "I can't think why he's not answering."

"Is the door locked?" Bette asked.

Rainey tried the knob. It wouldn't turn.

"We'll have to wait until he comes back or wakes up," Emily said.

"No we don't." Rainey reached up and took a cotter key from atop the door frame. "All the doors around here unlock this way."

"I always forget about those," Emily said.

Rainey slipped the angled bit of metal into the hole beneath the doorknob and they heard the lock pop.

Doug's room was dark and crowded, the blinds drawn and items piled on the floor, the bed and every flat surface—clothing, shoes, magazines, video games—and on a bookshelf by the door, a bottle of pine cleaner and a syringe. Bette stared at the items. "He must have injected the cakes with this," she said. "He could have even done it after I iced them. If he used just a little bit you wouldn't even be able to tell what he had done by looking."

Behind her, Rainey began to weep. "Why would he do something so horrible?" she sobbed. "Why would he ruin your beautiful cakes?"

The woman's distress moved Bette. She was angry about the ruined petit fours, but Rainey was devastated. "I don't blame you," she said. "Doug is responsible for his own actions."

"What are you going to do about the party?" Rainey asked.

"We have plenty of other food," Emily said. "I'm betting the sandwiches and cream puffs are all right."

"But the cakes—you have to have cake at a party," Rainey said. She sniffed and wiped her eyes. "I can help you make more. I'll do whatever you need me to do."

Bette considered the offer. "We don't have time to make more petit fours."

"We could make cupcakes," Rainey said. "They don't take long, and you could decorate them all fancy."

Bette nodded. "Cupcakes are a good idea." Not as impressive as petit fours, maybe, but the women would like them. She patted Rainey's arm. "Come on. Let's get to work. We have just enough time before Lacy's guests arrive."

"SURPRISED TO SEE you here, Cody," Dwight said as he entered Moe's Pub that evening and spotted the marshal at the end of the bar with Travis and Gage. "How are you feeling?"

"About like you'd expect someone to feel who's been shot and carved up." Cody wrapped his hand around a glass of iced tea. He would have preferred a stiff whiskey, but before leaving the ranch he had reluctantly taken one of the pain pills the doctor had prescribed and he knew better than to mix narcotics and alcohol.

"You could have stayed back at the ranch," Travis said.

"He didn't want to miss seeing you attempt to cut loose and enjoy yourself," Gage said.

Travis looked as if he wanted to cut something, all right. Or someone. "What's the plan for this evening?" he asked.

"I wanted to hire dancing girls, but you nixed that idea," Gage said.

"There are no dancing girls in Eagle Mountain," Dwight said. "What's plan B?"

"Plan B is to buy the groom a beer." He signaled to Moe, who was behind the bar. He slid over a pint and Gage handed it to Travis. "Then we have a little gift for you."

Cody and Bette had eventually gotten around to attaching the antlers to the stuffed cow—they poked out of the top of the shopping bag he handed to Travis. The sheriff set aside the pint glass and accepted the bag with the stoicism of a man who has resigned himself to eating a live worm. He pulled the cow out of the bag and his cheeks pinked. The rest of the men, who had already heard the story behind the gift, guffawed. "You never got a trophy from your first deer hunt," Gage said. "So we thought you deserved one now."

"You can hang it over the fireplace," one of the groomsmen, Ryder Stewart, said.

"Very funny." Travis set the cow aside and stood. "How about a game of pool?"

Someone put money in the jukebox, and most of the men teamed up to play pool at the two tables at the back of the room. Cody remained at the end of the bar, sipping tea and wondering if he would have been better off staying home. Gage slid onto the stool next to Cody. "You should have been the one to have a bachelor party," Cody said. "You would have enjoyed it more."

"Oh, Travis is having a good time." They watched as the sheriff bent over the pool table and lined up his cue. "He's a shark and this lets him show off his skills, plus I'm going to make sure he drinks more than he should. He needs to forget about this serial killer business for a while."

"Is he getting a lot of pressure from the town to solve the crime?"

"Eagle Mountain's new mayor thinks Travis hung the moon—but he doesn't need to apply any pressure. My brother is good at doing that himself."

"It's a tough case," Cody said.

"It is. We can't catch a break, and meanwhile, this guy goes around murdering more women." He set down his beer. "This conversation is too depressing. We need to talk about something else."

"Such as?"

"Such as—what's up with you and that pretty blonde caterer?"

"Bette."

"Yeah. Bette." Gage gave him the look of a cop interrogating a suspect. "Travis said you went to bat for her pretty hard over those stolen rings. You don't think she took them."

"Travis doesn't, either," Cody said. "Not really."

"Travis said she was pretty upset about you getting shot," Gage said.

"The guy was shooting at her, too. That would upset anybody."

"She was the first person you asked about when I picked you up this morning."

Cody sipped his tea. "Why are you interested in my personal life?"

"I'm a nosy guy. It's a good quality for a cop."

"Go nose into someone else's life."

Gage stood. "Maybe I will."

The door to the bar opened and a man stepped in. He scanned the room, taking in the half a dozen men playing pool and the two at the bar. A tall man with hunched shoulders, he had a few wisps of gray hair about his balding head and a ragged gray goatee. Moe moved from behind the bar. "This is a private party," he said. "Didn't you see the sign on the door?"

"It's okay, Moe." Cody put up his hand. He motioned to the newcomer. "Come on in. I'll buy you a drink."

The man hesitated, but apparently the prospect of a free drink won him over. He shambled to the bar and took the stool a few down from Cody. Moe had just served him a beer when Travis and Gage joined them. Travis slid onto the stool beside the man. "Hello, Carl," he said.

The man flinched. "Are you talking to me?"

"Carl Wayland, right?" Travis asked.

"I don't know anybody by that name." He turned his attention to his drink.

"How about Charlie Fergusen?"

"I'd better go." The man stood, but Gage put a hand on his shoulder. "Stay a minute and talk to us."

Carl looked around. All the men had gathered at the bar now. Dwight and Ryder still carried pool cues. "What is this?" he demanded. "Can't a man come in out of the cold and have a drink?"

"What are you doing in Eagle Mountain, Carl?" Travis asked, his tone genial.

"None of your business."

"Where are you staying since you checked out of the Eagle Mountain Inn?" Cody asked.

"Again—none of your business." He hunched over the bar and sipped his beer.

"Where were you yesterday afternoon?" Travis asked. "From, say, three o'clock until seven?"

Carl remained silent.

"What about Wednesday morning?" Cody asked. "Where were you then?"

Carl shoved back from the bar. "I gotta get out of here. It stinks too much of cop in this place."

He moved past Travis and Gage, but Cody blocked his exit. "Bette Fuller doesn't want to see you," he said. "If you come anywhere near her, I'll have you back in jail, charged with harassment."

Carl grinned, showing a broken incisor. "Bette is an old friend," he said. "A real nice girl. When you see her, you tell her I said hello." He pushed past Cody and out the door. Cody started to follow, but Travis held him back.

"I just want to get a look at his car," Cody said.

"Dwight is taking care of that," Travis said. "He's going to follow him and see where he's staying."

Of course Travis would have thought of that. Cody sat on the bar stool again.

Travis's phone rang. He answered it, turning slightly away from Cody and speaking low. Then he pocketed the phone and looked around the room. "Gage!"

Every head in the room swiveled toward the sheriff. There was no mistaking the urgency in his voice. Gage came over. "What's up?" he asked.

Travis voice was rough with strain. "There's been another woman killed," he said. "They found her in her car near the high school."

"To Lacy!" Maya held a glass of champagne aloft in a toast. "A wonderful friend who is going to be a beautiful bride, my future sister-in-law and a woman who knows how to throw a great party!"

"To Lacy!" the others echoed.

"Speech! Speech!" someone called.

Cheeks flushed with happiness—and maybe a little from the champagne—Lacy stood. "Thank you all so much for coming tonight," she said. "It's been so special for me to get to spend this time with all my favorite women in the world." She spread her arms wide, as if to give them all a hug, and they clapped.

Lacy gestured to the one vacant place at the tables. "I'm so sorry Paige wasn't able to be here. Everyone keep your fingers crossed that the highway opens again before the wedding."

"I ate her share of the refreshments," Emily said, to more laughter.

"Wasn't the food fantastic?" Lacy said. She held up her champagne glass. "I want to propose a toast to my friend Bette, who made this scrumptious feast."

"Thanks to Rainey, too," Bette said. "She helped a lot with the cupcakes." Together, Rainey and Bette had baked carrot cake and devil's food cupcakes, decorated with cream cheese or buttercream frosting, and decorated with hand-piped snowflakes.

"And now I have something else for you all," Lacy said. She beckoned to Bette, who came forward and began handing out little white boxes tied with silver ribbon. "These are just little thank-yous to all of you for being in my wedding. I appreciate each of you so much."

A beaming Casey held aloft the little crystal snowflake on a silver chain that Lacy had chosen for her.

The other women oohed and aahed over the jewelry they received while Bette rearranged the refreshment table, consolidating the food so it looked less picked-over, and removing empty trays and platters. There wasn't that much left, a sign that the women had enjoyed everything. Fortunately, the petit fours were the only casualty of Doug's tampering.

"Bette, come up here," Lacy said.

Bette turned, surprised. Lacy had retrieved a white gift bag from somewhere. "I have something for you, too," she said. "You didn't think I'd leave you out, did you?"

Feeling a little self-conscious, Bette walked over and accepted the gift bag. "Open it!" Emily called.

The bag contained a large box wrapped in silver paper. Bette lifted the lid of the box and gasped. "Lacy!" She lifted out a pristine chef's smock, her name in dark blue lettering on the left breast pocket. Beneath this was a pair of checked chef's pants. Tears stung Bette's eyes as she stroked the fabric.

"I remembered you saying how one day you wanted a real chef's outfit," Lacy said.

Yes, Bette had said that. But these items, the cut and quality of them, had been out of Bette's reach when she had so many other expenses associated with starting her catering business. "They're beautiful," she said.

The friends hugged, then retreated to the kitchen with the boxes. "That's a really nice gift," Rainey said, admiring the chef's coat. "You'll look real professional in them." She nodded toward the party. "Travis found himself a really nice young woman. I wasn't too sure at first, but then it goes to show I can be inclined to misjudge."

"I think we all do that," Bette said. She had misjudged Rainey, mistaking her insecurity for animosity and her concern for her son as involvement in his wrongdoing.

"Doug still hasn't come home," Rainey said. "It's not like him to be away so long. I guess he knows he's in big trouble over those petit fours."

"I had to tell Lacy what happened," Bette said. "And I'm sure she'll tell Travis. It's up to them what happens next."

Rainey nodded. "I wanted him here because I wanted to keep him out of trouble," she said. "I thought away from the city, he'd have less temptation. And this would be a good job to have on his résumé. I guess you know how it is—when you have a blot on your record, people never want to look past it. They don't even give you a chance."

"I know." Lacy had given Bette a chance—her wedding planner had already talked to Bette about catering another wedding for a client in Denver, and with a few more jobs like that, and good references, she would be on her way.

"The problem is, a young man who's used to the city life gets bored here in the country,"

Rainey continued. "There's not enough for him to do. And it's always been hard for Doug to make friends. He told me recently he ran into someone he knew from Denver, who was visiting Eagle Mountain, and that seemed to cheer him up. But I worry, you know? Maybe if his father had stayed around to be a good influence on him he would have had an easier time of it. Or if I'd stayed in Denver to keep a closer eye on him, but as soon as he was out of school, he was anxious to be out on his own, and the opportunity came to take this job with the Walkers—I didn't feel I could pass it up. They've been so good to me— I hope they don't blame me for what he's done."

"I'm sure they won't." Bette squeezed the older woman's arm. "I'll make sure they know you didn't have any part in this," she said.

Rainey sniffed and turned away. "They're still talking and eating in there," she said. "You have time to put your gift in your cabin. You don't want those nice things getting dirty. And really, I can handle cleaning up after them myself. I'll box up the leftovers and we can deal with the rest in the morning."

"Thanks. But I shouldn't be gone long." Bette grabbed her coat from the pegs by the back door and stepped outside. The moon was almost full and provided plenty of light for the walk to her cabin. The old snow crunched underfoot, but new flakes were beginning to fall, like a sifting of powdered sugar over an already-iced cake.

She reached the cabin and shifted the box to one arm so she could dig out her key. The new one the Walkers had given her when they changed the locks was attached to a key chain with a rabbit's foot—maybe they hoped this key would be luckier for her than the last one. She grabbed hold of the key chain and started to pull it out when a strong arm wrapped around her neck and dragged her back. She dropped the bag that contained the chef's outfit, the contents spilling across the welcome mat in front of her door. She tried to shout, but the arm around her neck tightened. "Hello again, Bette," a familiar voice growled in her ear. "Or should I say, goodbye."

Chapter Seventeen

Anita Allbritton was a short, plump woman of about forty, with strawberry blond hair and round, tortoise-shell glasses. She taught business technology and computer science at the high school, and worked summers at the local Humane Society thrift store. She drove a burnt-orange Toyota Yaris, and was discovered in the front seat of this vehicle in the high school parking lot by a parent who was picking up his son from a sleepover.

"I recognized Anita's car and thought it was odd it was parked way out on the edge of the lot like that," the very agitated man told Travis and Cody, who had insisted on coming with the sheriff to the scene. "I stopped to see if there was any kind of note or obvious sign of trouble." He swallowed, struggling for composure. "I couldn't believe when I looked inside and saw…saw…" He shook his head, unable to go on.

What he had seen was Anita Allbritton laid across the front seat of her vehicle, her throat cut and her wrists and ankles bound with duct tape. Travis had found the Ice Cold Killer's card in the ashtray of the car, and a bloodstain beside a dumpster behind the school that he thought indicated the kill site. The car itself was clean of evidence.

"It almost looks like it was just vacuumed," Gage said, studying the vehicle's gray carpeting. "Do you think he did that—took the time to vacuum it out?"

"Maybe." Travis looked around the lot. "There are no lights this far out. No games or other activities tonight. Not a lot of traffic on the road. The killer may have felt he could take his time, be more careful. It was just chance that the parents decided to meet here to pick up the kids from that birthday sleepover. Just chance that the dad drove over to take a look."

"You don't think he's the killer?" Gage asked.

Travis shook his head. "He had his two children in the car with him. We'll confirm the time he left his house with his wife, but I'm pretty sure it will check out." The man had been devastated by the discovery, and had vomited on the edge of the parking lot. Fortunately, by the time Travis questioned him, he had pulled himself together and was anxious to get his children away from there.

Deputy Jamie Douglass, an attractive young woman with long dark hair worn in a bun beneath the regulation Stetson, joined them. "I talked with the Delaneys," she said. "They're the parents who met Mr. Karnack here to drop off his son, Colin. They didn't even notice the car parked over here. They live on the other side of town. They chose the high school as a good place to meet because it's halfway between the two homes."

Travis surveyed the area. The school was flanked on three sides by empty pasture. Across the street the school district's bus barn and maintenance sheds were deserted. "There's a neighborhood behind the bus barn," Travis said. "Start knocking on doors over there. Maybe someone was driving by here and saw something."

"Yes, sir." Jamie shoved her hands into the pockets of her Sherpa-lined leather jacket. "I'm sorry I had to break up your bachelor party with something like this," she said.

"You weren't interrupting anything," Travis said. "Whenever I'm not working on this case, I'm thinking about it—and dreading the next call about a dead woman." He looked at the

Yaris. "It was only a matter of time. We aren't even managing to slow him down."

"Maybe we'll catch a break this time and someone saw something," Jamie said. "I'll get right on it."

"What can I do to help?" Cody asked, when she was gone.

"Go back to the ranch," Travis said. "Tell the women at Lacy's party to spend the night there. We have plenty of room. I don't want any of them out driving around tonight. And I'll feel a lot better if there's at least one cop there with them."

"Of course." Cody hesitated, then said, "Don't let this eat at you. You're doing everything you can to catch this guy—he's just not giving you anything to work with."

Travis studied the toes of his boots. "They tell you in the academy not to take the job personally. Maybe that works in the city, but in a small town like Eagle Mountain, everything is personal. I knew almost every one of these victims—some better than others, but they're all my responsibility. I wasn't just hired by the town—the citizens of this county elected me to do a job. There's no way to do that job except by taking it personally."

"It's why you're good at it," Cody said.

Travis swore—something Cody had never

heard him do. "I'm not good at it right now," he said. "If I was, I would have caught this guy—or guys—by now."

There was no sense arguing about it, Cody thought. In Travis's position, he would feel the same way. Though he could have told Travis that sense of responsibility wasn't limited to small-town cops. As much as Cody had tried to deny it in the weeks since it had happened, he felt responsible for the man who had killed himself in front of him. The man might be the worst kind of criminal—one who preyed on young children. But Cody's job had been to bring him to justice. When the guy pulled the trigger on that gun, he had cheated his victims and their families of that justice. He had prevented Cody from doing his job.

The drive to the ranch on the narrow mountain road seemed to take forever. Snow was falling again, and the cold seeped through Cody's clothes and the layer of bandages to his wound, until he felt like a giant was gripping him with strong fingers and squeezing, hard. The pain pill he had taken before the party had long since worn off. All he could do was grit his teeth and clench the steering wheel with one hand and keep pushing forward.

At the ranch, the women were gathered in the living room, donning coats and exchanging hugs. They stopped talking when Cody walked in and turned to look at him. "Cody, you're white as a sheet," Mrs. Walker exclaimed. "Come sit down before you fall down."

He shook his head. "Ladies, I have some news," he said. He looked for Bette in the crowd but didn't find her. She was probably in the kitchen, cleaning up after the party. "I'm afraid there's been another murder, a teacher from the school."

"Who?" It was Maya who spoke. She pushed her way to the front of the group. "Cody, please tell me," she said. "You're talking about one of my coworkers."

"Anita Allbritton." He looked at them sternly. "That information doesn't leave this room. The sheriff hasn't had time to notify her family."

"Poor Anita," Maya moaned. "How horrible."

"Travis wants you all to stay here tonight," he said. "We'd feel better if you weren't out on the roads tonight."

"Of course," Mrs. Walker said. "We have plenty of room."

"It'll be like a slumber party," Lacy said. "We'll find night things for you to wear—and we still have a couple of bottles of champagne and more food."

They moved away from the door, removing

coats and talking all at once about this latest turn of events. A group clustered about Maya, asking about Anita, while Emily and Brenda conferred with Lacy and Mrs. Walker about sleeping arrangements. Cody interrupted them. "Where's Bette?" he asked.

"In the kitchen, probably," Lacy said. She smiled. "The party turned out so wonderful. It was a real triumph."

"I'll let her know what's going on," he said and made his way to the kitchen.

Rainey was alone in the room, arranging leftover sandwiches in plastic storage containers. She looked up at his arrival. "Hello," she said. "What can I do for you?"

"Is Bette here?" he asked.

"No, she isn't. She left a little while ago to put something away in her cabin and she hasn't come back yet. I told her I didn't mind cleaning up after the party and I guess she decided to take me up on the offer."

"That doesn't sound like her, leaving you to do the work," Cody said.

"Well, no, it doesn't. But maybe she was tired. She worked really hard today." She yawned. "So did I."

"I'll stop by her cabin and check on her," Cody said. He moved past her to the back door, quickening his pace as he stepped into the snow. He told himself the latest murder had raised his anxiety level, but he couldn't shake the sense that something was really wrong. By the time he could see the row of cabins ahead, he had broken into a painful jog, every movement jarring his injured shoulder.

The scene didn't look right. Something was scattered across the porch of Bette's cabin. He bounded up the steps and stared at the gift bag, a box wrapped in torn silver paper, and what looked like a top and a pair of pants spilling across the doormat. A gift? But what was it doing here?

He stepped over the items and pounded on the door. "Bette! Bette, it's me, Cody!"

He pressed his ear to the door but heard nothing inside. He tried the knob, but the door was locked—and Bette was the only one with a key to the new lock.

He forced himself to step back, to slow down and examine the scene objectively—to think like the cop he was. He studied the items strewn across the doormat. They hadn't been placed— they had been dropped. Bette had been standing here in front of the door, maybe searching for her key, and something had made her drop the package. Surprise? Fear?

He retraced his path to the steps and studied the snow illuminated in the moonlight.

The snow here was churned up, then dug into grooves. A struggle, then someone being dragged backward, the person's heels digging in. Heart pounding, he followed the marks until they stopped, beside the track from a vehicle.

He squatted down and studied the impressions, still fairly clear despite a light dusting of snow. Deep tread on wide tires. But not car or truck tires. They were too close together. They were tractor tires—or no, tires of one of the utility vehicles used around the ranch for everything from hauling hay to plowing snow to herding cattle.

That meant that whoever took Bette was probably still on the ranch. Cody pulled out his phone and called Travis. "I'm here at the ranch and Bette is missing," he told the sheriff. "Looks like someone grabbed her on the front porch of her cabin. I found the tracks of what looks like a utility vehicle. I'm going to follow them."

"Wait for me," Travis said. "I can be there in thirty minutes."

"I don't have time to wait," Cody said. "The snow is covering the tracks fast." And he didn't know what whoever took her planned to do with Bette. He might already be too late. "Where is Carl? Is Dwight still with him?"

"Dwight followed him to a rental out of town,

then he returned to help process the scene at the high school."

Carl could have hurt Bette. "I have to go after them now," Cody said.

"Get one of the ranch hands to go with you," Travis said. "Or more than one."

"I don't have time to go looking for people," he said. "Besides, it's Saturday night. They might not even be here. They're probably in town, or visiting family or friends."

Snow was falling harder. "I have to go," he said. "You can track me when you get here." He ended the call and stowed his phone, then pulled his coat more tightly around him and set off across the snow, following the line of treads that led over the pasture.

BETTE LAY ON the floor of the old cabin where the sleighing party had gathered. Was that really only two days ago? Duct tape tightly bound her hands and feet, and a bone-deep chill had seeped in, so that her teeth kept chattering—or maybe that was just fear.

Carl sat on an upturned section of log across from her. "I bet you never thought you'd see me again," he said. He chuckled, a sound like an accordion with a hole in the bellows. "Get it, 'Bette'?"

"Why are you doing this, Carl?" she asked. "What did I ever do to you?"

"Oh, it's nothing personal, sweetheart. I'm just doing a favor for an old friend. He needs you out of the way before you open your big mouth."

"You mean Eddie." She'd known it, hadn't she? As much as she told herself she had nothing to worry about, that Eddie wouldn't waste any more time on her, she'd been fooling herself.

"Eddie?" Carl laughed again. "Not him. He's dead."

"Dead?"

"Yeah. Got knifed in an alley one night just a couple weeks after he got out." Carl shrugged. "Guess he crossed the wrong guy."

"I don't understand," she said. "If you're not doing this for Eddie…"

"You don't think I have more than one friend?"

Stamping footsteps on the porch interrupted him. The door opened and Doug Whittington came in, brushing snow off the shoulders of his coat. "We could have picked a better night for this," he said.

"Doug, what are you doing?" Bette asked.

He scowled at her. "What do you think we're doing? We're going to slit your throat, stick you in your car and drive you out to some deserted road. By the time the cops find you, Carl and I will be safely tucked in our beds—innocent lambs who don't know anything about what happened to you."

"You're the Ice Cold Killer?" She hated the way her voice shook on the words.

"No!" Doug shook his head. "But that's who the cops will think did you." He felt around in his pockets and handed Carl a small white card. "This is why I was late. I had to wait until the coast was clear so I could sneak into the Walkers' home office and print this."

Carl showed Bette the card, which read "Ice Cold." "It's genius, right?" he said.

"It's a stupid catering job!" she said. "That's not worth killing me over."

He walked over to her and stood looking down. "You really don't know who I am, do you?" he asked. He picked up one of the kerosene lanterns and held it closer to his face. "Sure I don't look familiar?"

She stared, recognition washing over her like a bucket of cold water. "You drove the getaway car," she whispered.

"Bingo." He set the lantern down. "I couldn't have you telling the police that, could I? They don't just want me for my part in the bank robbery—they want to hang me for the murder of that pedestrian. It wasn't my fault the dope walked out in front of me!"

"But I didn't remember it was you!" she said. "I couldn't have told the police anything."

"You'd have figured it out soon enough," Doug said. "I couldn't keep avoiding you all the time. Not with my mom nagging me about helping her more in the kitchen, and you always popping in and out of there. It's your own fault we're having to take such drastic measures, you know."

"What do you mean?" she asked.

"I tried to warn you off," he said. "I left that message on your door—I even hit you in the head with that rock. I thought you'd believe you'd narrowly escaped being the Ice Cold Killer's next victim and you'd want to get out of Dodge, wedding or no wedding."

"You stole the wedding rings and planted them in my room," she said.

He frowned. "I thought the sheriff would carry you off to jail and that would be the last we saw of you. It was really tempting to keep those rings for myself, but I figured that was working a little too close to home. But then that marshal had to stick his nose in things and I finally accepted that I wasn't going to scare you off. I was going to have to do something more drastic."

"That's where I come in," Carl said. "A job like this works better with two people."

"So he called you to come out and help kill me," she said.

"Not exactly," Carl said. "I actually looked him up. I wanted to see about doing another job together. He told me about his problem with you and I offered to help him out."

"Which one of you tampered with the snowmobile and shot at Cody and me?" she asked.

"That was me," Carl said. "I should have just picked you off while you were sitting out there on the ice, but I wanted to make it a little more fun. I almost had you, too. A few more minutes and the marshal was bound to run out of ammo, then I would have closed in for the kill." He frowned. "Too bad I didn't finish off the marshal when I had the chance. I would have liked to have taken out a fed."

Bette looked at Doug. "You're being stupid," she said. "You'll never get away with this."

"Who are you calling stupid? I'm the only one involved in that bank job that didn't get caught. I've been walking around free while you did eight years. Besides, Travis and his buddies think I'm just some jealous punk. They think poisoning your fancy cakes is as malicious as I get." He reached down and took her arm. "Come on. We need to go."

He lifted her by the arms, while Carl hefted her legs. They carried her out to the utility vehicle and dumped her in the bed. She had to lie with her knees to her chin to fit. "This snow is perfect," Carl said. "It will cover up our tracks. Did you get her car keys?"

"I got them," Doug said. "I had to break the back window to get in. The key I had for the door to her cabin doesn't work anymore. They must have changed the locks after the business with the rings."

"I told you that was never going to work," Carl said. "You should have just kept the rings for yourself. That gold is worth a lot these days. We could have melted it down and no one would ever know."

"Yeah, well, it's too late now." Doug climbed in beside him. "Let's get this over with."

Carl started the vehicle and it jolted forward. Bette tried to sit up. If she could lean out over the back, maybe she could fall out.

And then what? It wasn't as if she could run away, or even crawl, trussed up as she was. She closed her eyes and tried to pray. Surely someone from the ranch house had missed her by now—Lacy, or even Rainey. What time would Cody and the others return from Travis's party? Probably not until late. Too late for her.

"What the—!" The vehicle skidded sharply

to the right as gunshots sounded. Bette flattened herself to the bed of the cargo area, flinching as a bullet thudded into the side of the vehicle.

"It's that marshal!" Doug shouted. He—or maybe Carl, Bette couldn't be sure—returned fire.

"Come on!" Doug shouted. "He's on foot. He can't catch up with us."

"I'm going as fast as I can," Carl said. "It's not that easy in this snow."

Another bullet struck the vehicle, this time hitting the tailgate, inches from Bette's curled legs. She had to let Cody know she was in here, before he accidentally shot her.

Grunting with the effort, she sat up, praying Cody would see her. She looked back and spotted him, pounding after the utility vehicle, his gun in his uninjured hand. But he was no longer firing. He had seen her; she was sure of it.

The vehicle jounced over rough ground, throwing her back against the tailgate. One of the men fired at Cody, but the shot was wild. She wondered if they were even aiming—if it was possible to aim in the wildly careening vehicle.

She jolted against the tailgate again, and one side of the latch popped. Sitting up again, she braced herself against the side of cargo bed and slammed both feet into the other end of the latch. It gave way and, afraid of losing her nerve if she waited, she rolled out of the vehicle.

She hit the ground hard, but the thick snow provided some cushion. She forced herself to keep rolling, despite the pain of every movement, trying to put as much distance between herself and her two captors as possible.

Cody stopped her, dropping to his knees beside her. "I'm here," he gasped, trying to catch his breath.

She lay still, tears freezing on her cheeks. "What are they doing?" she asked.

"They're coming back."

"They'll kill us," she said.

"No." He crouched in front of her and fired toward the approaching vehicle. They returned the fire, but as before, their shots went wild. Cody kept firing, a rapid burst of staccato reports. Bette closed her eyes and waited—for what, she wasn't sure.

And then she realized the sound of the utility vehicle's motor was fading. And Cody had stopped shooting. "They're running away," he said.

He holstered his weapon, then found a knife and began cutting away the layers of tape around her wrists and ankles. He helped her sit up, rubbing her hands between his own to restore her circulation. She cupped his face and kissed him. They held each other for a long moment, neither of them speaking.

"Come on," he said finally. "Let's get out of here before we freeze to death." He stood and helped her to her feet, then, leaning on each other, they started walking toward the ranch house.

Travis and Gage met them when they were halfway home, pulling up on snowmobiles. "Carl Wayland and Doug Whittington are in one of the ranch utility vehicles," Cody said. "I'm pretty sure I wounded both of them. They had kidnapped Bette and they tried to kill both of us."

"They were going to kill me and make it look like another murder by the Ice Cold Killer," Bette said. "Doug even printed up a business card on your home office printer."

"We need to go after them," Travis said. "Can you make it back to the ranch house?"

"Go," Cody said. "We'll be fine."

By the time they reached the house, Bette was shaking with cold and Cody's breath hissed through his teeth with each step. The man had just gotten out of the hospital this morning— how had he even found the strength to come after her?

The women who had attended the party descended on them with blankets and steaming mugs of cocoa and hot water bottles, then Lacy shooed them all away. "Don't bombard them with questions," she said. "Let them catch their breaths."

Bette and Cody huddled together on the sofa. When Bette had finally stopped shaking, she asked, "Do you think Travis and Gage will find Carl and Doug?"

"They'll find them," he said.

"Doug admitted he wrote that message on my door," she said. "And he stole the rings and planted them in my room. And he was the one who attacked me that day on the road. Carl was the one who tampered with the snowmobile and shot at us."

Cody sipped his cocoa. "Why did they go after you?" he asked.

"Doug was the getaway driver in the robbery. The one who killed that pedestrian. I didn't recognize him, but he had never let me get a really good look at him. Once I saw him in good light, I realized who he was. He was afraid I'd turn him in and he'd go to prison for robbery and for killing that man."

"Where does Carl come in?"

"He came to town to ask Doug to do a job with him. I think he meant another robbery.

Doug told him about me and they decided they needed to get rid of me. Permanently."

She laced her fingers in his. "Thanks to you, that didn't happen."

He turned to look at her. "I think I'm going to have to take you into protective custody," he said.

Her heart skipped a beat. "What are you talking about?"

He brought their linked hands to his lips, kissing her knuckles. "One of my jobs as a US marshal is witness protection," he said. "I think I need to put you under my protection. Permanently."

She caught her breath. "You're going to have to speak plainer than that, Marshal."

"I'm asking you to marry me," he said. "I love you and tonight I learned that I don't really want to live without you."

She thought of him, facing down that vehicle racing toward him, bullets flying. He had done that to protect her. To protect what they had found together. "Can a US marshal marry someone with a criminal record?" she asked.

"I don't care if they can or not," he said. "I want to marry you. If you'll have me."

"I'll have you." She kissed his cheek. "But your job—"

"I'm on leave for at least three months, with

my injured shoulder. And since I've come here, I've been thinking. Maybe it's time for a change."

"What will you do if you're not a marshal?"

"I have a law degree. All I have to do is pass the bar and I can study for that while I recuperate. What would you think of being married to an attorney?"

"Defense or prosecution?"

"Prosecution. I can leave law enforcement, but I can't leave putting away criminals."

"Fair enough."

He squeezed her hand. "So your answer is yes?"

"Yes. I'll marry you." She kissed him, then couldn't stop smiling. "You know, I have a fabulous recipe for wedding cake."

"I can't wait to taste it."

"By the time we caught up with Carl and Doug, they were ready to surrender," Travis said over breakfast the next morning. "They had wrecked the ute and were both freezing, and bleeding pretty heavily." He glanced at Cody, who sat across from Travis at the table, next to Bette. "You hit Doug once and Carl twice. None of the shots were serious, though Carl has a broken arm. I've got two deputies guarding them at the clinic. As soon as the doctor will release them, we'll lock them up in our holding cell until we can transfer them to Junction."

"We found that business card on Doug," Gage said. "Too bad we couldn't get them for the Ice Cold murders, too."

"They couldn't have done those murders," Travis said. "Carl was talking to us at Moe's when Anita was killed. He was in Denver when Kelly and Christi died, and Doug was here at the ranch."

"How is Rainey taking the news about Doug?" Lacy asked.

"She's stoic," Travis said. "Blaming herself, I think."

"I imagine she's heartbroken," Bette said. "He's really all she has. She told me she raised him pretty much on her own after his father deserted them."

"I'm glad he's gone," Lacy said. "Poisoning those cakes was downright creepy, and then when I learned all he did to you—well, it was horrible."

"We caught him on camera taking the spare key to the old lock on your cabin yesterday afternoon," Travis said. "And we have the gun Carl used when he shot at you two. We shouldn't have any trouble sending both of them to prison for a long time, on multiple counts."

"Any news on Anita's murder?" Cody asked.

"No." Travis poked at his eggs with a fork, his expression glum. "All we can do is keep looking."

"You'll find the killer," Lacy said. "If anyone can, you will."

"Spoken like a loving bride," Bette said.

"Of course." She looked at each of them in turn. "I'm not being callous, but in spite of this killer, we have a wedding to prepare for," she said. "In the midst of so much tragedy, it's especially important to hold on to the joyous occasions."

Bette lifted her glass of orange juice. "Here, here," she said.

Lacy's smile grew sly. "I hear you have some joyous news of your own," she said.

Bette looked at Cody, who cleared his throat. "Bette and I are going to be married," he said.

"Congratulations," Travis said. "Though it's no surprise."

"No?" Cody asked.

"I figured you were pretty much gone after that first day." He glanced at Lacy. "I know the signs from personal experience."

"We haven't set the date yet," Bette said. "It will be after we're settled again in Denver, but you'll all be invited to the wedding, I promise."

"If I were you, I'd wait until that shoulder

heals," Gage said. "Be a shame to have to deal with that on your honeymoon."

"I don't know about that." Bette rubbed Cody's uninjured shoulder. "This way, I have the upper hand. Not a position I've ever been in with a US marshal."

"Watch yourself," Cody said. "Even with one hand tied behind my back—so to speak—I can get the best of you."

"I don't know about that," Lacy said. "It looks to me as if Bette has pulled off one last heist."

Cody's eyes narrowed. "Oh?"

Lacy laughed. "Yeah, you goof. Clearly, she's stolen your heart."

Everyone around the table groaned, but Cody's eyes met Bette's, and she thought she could never get tired of looking into those depths, figuring out what made this man tick. "Guilty as charged," she said. Lacy was right. In spite of all the tragedy around them, it was important to celebrate the things in life worth hanging on to. Like the kind of love that gave you infinite second chances.

* * * * *

*Look for more books in Cindi Myers's
Eagle Mountain Murder Mystery:
Winter Storm Wedding miniseries
later in 2019.*

And don't miss the previous title in the series:

Ice Cold Killer

Available now from Harlequin Intrigue!